FOSSIL

Pleistocene human skull

Eocene gastropods

Eocene fish

Cretaceous dinosaur
finger bones

Triassic swimming reptile

Jurassic brittlestar

Cretaceous
cone (sectioned
and polished)

Cretaceous cone

Ordovician nautiloid
(polished and shaped)

Jurassic sea urchin

Carboniferous
horsetail

Modern
horsetail

Eocene
shark
tooth

Pleistocene coral

Carboniferous
fern

Jurassic ammonite
(carved as a
snakestone)

DK EYEWITNESS BOOKS

FOSSIL

Written by
PAUL D. TAYLOR, Ph.D.

Triassic
dinosaur
footprint

Carboniferous
lycopod

Eocene fish

Silurian
brachiopod

Pleistocene
handaxe

Permian tree fern
(sectioned and
polished)

Modern
coral

Pliocene scallop

Pleistocene
coral

DK

Dorling Kindersley

Cretaceous
dinosaur tooth

Jurassic
ammonite

Cretaceous bryozoan

Jurassic coral (sectioned
and polished)

Carboniferous spider

Pleistocene sea urchin

Cretaceous
opalized
gastropod

Cretaceous
opalized bivalve

Cretaceous worm tube

Miocene corals

DK

Dorling Kindersley

LONDON, NEW YORK, AUCKLAND, DELHI, JOHANNESBURG, MUNICH,
PARIS and SYDNEY

For a full catalog, visit

 www.dk.com

Project Editor Louise Pritchard
Art Editor Alison Anholt-White
Senior Editor Sophie Mitchell
Senior Art Editor Julia Harris
Editorial Director Sue Unstead
Art Director Anne-Marie Bulat
Special photography Colin Keates
(Natural History Museum, London)

© 1990 Dorling Kindersley Limited
This edition © 2000 Dorling Kindersley Limited
First American edition, 1990

Published in the United States by
Dorling Kindersley Publishing, Inc.
95 Madison Avenue
New York, NY 10016
2 4 6 8 10 9 7 5 3 1

Dorling Kindersley books are available at special discounts for bulk purchases for sales
promotions or premiums. Special editions, including personalized covers, excerpts of existing
guides, and corporate imprints can be created in large quantities for specific needs. For more
information, contact Special Markets Dept., Dorling Kindersley Publishing, Inc.,
95 Madison Ave., New York, NY 10016; Fax: (800) 600-9098

Library of Congress Cataloging-in-Publication Data
Taylor, Paul D.
Fossil / written by Paul D. Taylor;
photography by Colin Keates.
p. cm. — (Eyewitness Books)
Includes index.
Summary: A photo essay about different types of fossils,
from bacteria and algae to birds and mammals.
1. Paleontology — Juvenile literature.
[1. Fossils. 2. Paleontology.] I. Title.
QE714.5.T39 2000 560—dc20 89-36444
ISBN 0-7894-5841-1 (pb)
ISBN 0-7894-5840-3 (hc)

Color reproduction by Colourscan, Singapore
Printed in China by Toppan Printing Co. (Shenzhen) Ltd.

Pleistocene
gastropods

Silurian
sea lily

Miocene bat jaws

19th-century
microscope for
examining thin
sections

Slide of thin section of
Carboniferous bryozoans

Modern
magnolia flower

Contents

Jurassic
ammonites

Silurian trilobite
(mounted as a brooch)

Fossils-true and false

FOSSILS ARE THE REMAINS or evidence of animals or plants that have been preserved naturally. They range in size from huge dinosaur skeletons to tiny plants and animals which can only be seen under a microscope. Most fossils are formed from the hard parts of animals and plants, such as shells, bones, teeth, or wood. They may be virtually unchanged from the originals, or they may be mineral replacements. Animals and plants have also been preserved in peat, tar, ice, and amber, the resin of ancient trees. Eggs, footprints, and burrows can be fossilized too. The study of fossils, called paleontology, shows us that life originated on Earth at least 3,500 million years ago. Since then there has been a succession of animal and plant species. Most are now extinct, and only a tiny number have survived as fossils. By studying these survivors, we can get a fascinating glimpse of ancient life on Earth.

WHAT CAN IT BE?
Although people have been collecting fossils for hundreds of years, the true nature of them was a mystery until relatively recently. This illustration appeared in an Italian book published in 1670.

ONLY BONES
Bones are often the only remains of animals because they are the hardest parts. This is the fossilized vertebra from the backbone of an ancient, giant swimming reptile called a plesiosaur (pp. 46–47).

Trilobite cast and mold

TAKING SHAPE
Fossils are often found in two parts. Sometimes, after burial, an animal rots away, and leaves a hollow mold. If the mold is then filled by sediment (p. 9) it may harden to form a cast.

Plesiosaur tooth

HARD TOOTH
Teeth are often found as fossils, as they are made of hard material.

RARE DELICACY
Detailed fossils of plants are rare because they rot away quickly when they die. In this leaf, however, even the delicate veins have been preserved.

PEARLY AMMONITE
The mollusks known as ammonites (pp. 28-29) are now extinct. They had hard shells made of a chalky mineral called aragonite, with a colorful outer layer of mother-of-pearl. This one has been preserved almost in its original state.

PRECIOUS WOOD
One kind of fossilization occurs when chemical changes cause a mineral to grow, grain by grain, in place of the original tissues of the animal or plant. The tissues of this fossilized wood have been replaced by opal.

ANCIENT TRAIL
This is the trail of an unknown animal which moved across the sea bed millions of years ago. Fossilized evidence of the activities of an animal, like this trail, is called a trace fossil.

UNNATURAL BURIAL
This ancient Greek pot, discovered buried in the ground, is not a fossil. In the past the term *fossil*, which means "something dug up," was used to describe many things found in the ground, such as ancient pottery and minerals, but these are no longer thought of as fossils.

Area where fragments are missing

FALSE FOSSIL
This is not a fossil. The tree like growths, called dendrites, are manganese that seeped into the rock.

Flint "duck's head"

EASY MISTAKE
These are not a fossilized duck's head and a human leg! Their shape is pure chance. They are really lumps of rock called flint nodules, found in chalk (p. 9). The shapes of flint nodules can be very peculiar and are often mistaken for fossils.

Flint "human leg"

ANIMAL OR VEGETABLE?
No - minerals! Minerals are not the remains of an animal or plant, and therefore they are not fossils.

Bunch of grapes

Squid-like creature

PACKED TIGHT
Sometimes fossils are found densely packed because the animals lived in great numbers. These small ammonites are in limestone (p. 9).

FOSSIL FAKES
During the 1720s, at a time when the nature of fossils was unclear, these "fossils" were carved and buried in the ground by people who wanted to fool a scientist named Johann Beringer. He was taken in by the joke and published descriptions of his find which resulted in his humiliation when the hoax was uncovered.

Beringer's "Lying Stones"

The making of rocks

AMETHYST
This is the purple variety of the mineral quartz. If allowed to grow freely, quartz crystals are pointed and hexagonal (six-sided).

THE MANY KINDS OF ROCKS beneath our feet have been forming for more than 4,000 million years. The Earth's crust is made up of elements. The important ones are oxygen, silicon, aluminum, iron, calcium, sodium, potassium, magnesium, and carbon. These combine in different ways to form minerals. All rocks are made up of minerals. Common rock-forming minerals include calcite (calcium carbonate), quartz (silicon dioxide), and feldspars (complex minerals containing aluminum, silicon, calcium, sodium, and potassium). There are three groups of rocks: igneous, metamorphic, and sedimentary.

FOLDED ROCK
Powerful movements in the Earth's crust can cause rocks to crack and form faults, or to buckle, creating folds like this.

Feldspar *Mica* *Quartz*

Black mica
Glassy quartz
White feldspar

Thin section of granite

Distorted trilobite

TWISTED TRILOBITE
Metamorphic rocks may contain distorted fossils such as this trilobite (p. 30) in slate.

GRANITE
The speckles in this granite are individual minerals. Granite is an igneous rock formed at great depths.

Molten rocks

Igneous rocks are formed by the cooling of molten magma (liquid rock) from deep within the Earth. Sometimes the magma reaches the surface and erupts from volcanoes as lava before it cools. Most often, though, the magma cools and becomes solid deep underground.

LAYER UPON LAYER
The Grand Canyon in Arizona, formed by the erosion of sandstone and limestone, is a natural slice through the Earth's crust. The oldest stratum, or layer, is at the bottom, the youngest at the top.

Band rich in mica

Band rich in quartz

SCHIST
Parallel banding of minerals is a common feature of metamorphic rocks. Schist is formed from shale or mud.

Changed rocks

High temperatures and pressures can change rocks into new types called metamorphic rocks. Marble is a metamorphosed limestone; slate, a metamorphosed shale.

Band of quartz

Band of silicate minerals

Thin section of schist

One varve
Fine sediment
Coarse sediment

ROCK BANDS
Stratification on a much smaller scale than the Grand Canyon is seen in this sedimentary rock. Each set of one light layer (fine sediment) and one dark layer (coarse sediment) is a year's accumulation of silt and mud, called a varve, at the bottom of a glacier-fed lake. Such well-defined seasonal bands are rare.

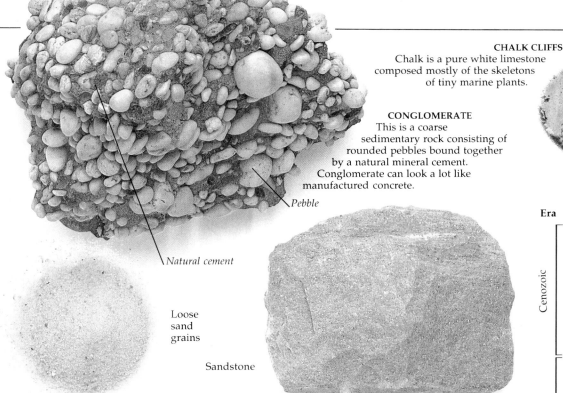

CHALK CLIFFS
Chalk is a pure white limestone composed mostly of the skeletons of tiny marine plants.

CONGLOMERATE
This is a coarse sedimentary rock consisting of rounded pebbles bound together by a natural mineral cement. Conglomerate can look a lot like manufactured concrete.

Pebble

Natural cement

Loose sand grains

Sandstone

Deposited rocks

Rocks are continually being eroded, creating grains which are carried by rivers, by the sea, and by the wind. These grains are deposited, together with the remains of animals and plants, as mud, sand, or coarser material. As this sediment is buried deeper by more sediment, it is compacted (pressed down) and cemented by the growth of minerals to form a sedimentary rock. Sandstone, for example, is a sedimentary rock made from cemented sand.

Quartz

Iron-rich cement

Thin section of sandstone

FROM ROCK TO ROCK
As cliffs of sedimentary rocks are eroded, small pieces of rock are deposited on the beach. These will be eroded further and may eventually form new sedimentary rock.

Shell fragment

Thin section of limestone

Finely broken shells

FOSSIL CONTAINER
Many sedimentary rocks contain hard lumps called concretions or nodules. These were formed after the sediment was deposited, often around fossil shells like this clam (p. 26).

Clam shell

FOSSILIFEROUS ROCK
Limestone is a sedimentary rock composed mainly of calcite and a few other similar carbonate minerals. The calcite is usually derived from the broken shells and skeletons of animals and plants that lived in the sea. Larger, more intact shells can also be present, and limestones are therefore good rocks in which to hunt for fossils. This Silurian limestone contains some fossil brachiopods (pp. 24–25).

Fossil brachiopod

Era	Period	Million years ago (mya)
Cenozoic	Holocene (epoch)	0.01
Cenozoic	Pleistocene (epoch)	2
Cenozoic	Pliocene (epoch)	5
Cenozoic	Miocene (epoch)	25
Cenozoic	Oligocene (epoch)	38
Cenozoic	Eocene (epoch)	55
Cenozoic	Paleocene (epoch)	65
Mesozoic	Cretaceous	144
Mesozoic	Jurassic	213
Mesozoic	Triassic	248
Paleozoic	Permian	286
Paleozoic	Carboniferous	360
Paleozoic	Devonian	408
Paleozoic	Silurian	438
Paleozoic	Ordovician	505
Paleozoic	Cambrian	590
	Precambrian (about seven times longer than all the other periods put together)	4,600 (origin of the Earth)

STRATIGRAPHICAL COLUMN
A series of eras and periods (and epochs in the Cenozoic) are used to describe the age of rocks and fossils.

Turning to stone

THE PROCESS OF CHANGING from a living organism to a fossil takes place over millions of years. Fossilization is an extremely chancy process. As soon as animals and plants die, they begin to decompose, or rot. The hard parts – the shells, bones, and teeth of animals; the wood of plants – last longer than soft tissue but are often scattered by animals, wind, or flowing water. In order for something to be fossilized it must be buried quickly before it decomposes, usually by sediment such as sand or mud washed down by water. Some fossils later dissolve; others may be changed chemically or distorted and twisted out of shape by high temperatures and pressures. Only a tiny fraction will survive to be found. The mussel is a good example to show how something can be fossilized.

LAND SHAPES
Over millions of years rocks are eroded and re-shaped, bringing ancient fossils to the surface.

2 DECAYING MUSSEL
When the mussel dies, the two chalky shells open out like butterfly wings. The soft parts of the mussel enclosed by the shells soon begin to rot or are eaten by scavenging animals.

Living mussel

Byssal threads

1 LIVING MUSSEL
Mussels live attached to rocks and other hard surfaces in the sea by byssal threads. The soft parts are enclosed by two chalky shells. Each mussel may spend its entire life in one place, and dense masses form mussel beds. If a mussel becomes detached it may die, especially if it is swept into a different environment.

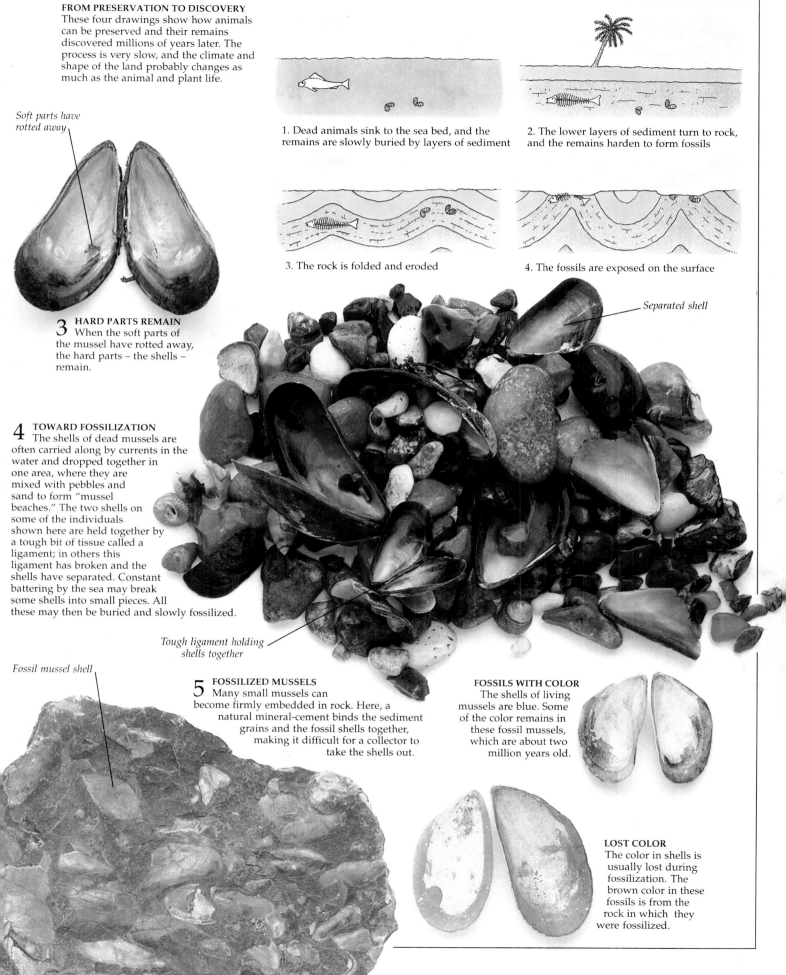

FROM PRESERVATION TO DISCOVERY
These four drawings show how animals can be preserved and their remains discovered millions of years later. The process is very slow, and the climate and shape of the land probably changes as much as the animal and plant life.

1. Dead animals sink to the sea bed, and the remains are slowly buried by layers of sediment

2. The lower layers of sediment turn to rock, and the remains harden to form fossils

3. The rock is folded and eroded

4. The fossils are exposed on the surface

Soft parts have rotted away

Separated shell

3 HARD PARTS REMAIN
When the soft parts of the mussel have rotted away, the hard parts – the shells – remain.

4 TOWARD FOSSILIZATION
The shells of dead mussels are often carried along by currents in the water and dropped together in one area, where they are mixed with pebbles and sand to form "mussel beaches." The two shells on some of the individuals shown here are held together by a tough bit of tissue called a ligament; in others this ligament has broken and the shells have separated. Constant battering by the sea may break some shells into small pieces. All these may then be buried and slowly fossilized.

Tough ligament holding shells together

Fossil mussel shell

5 FOSSILIZED MUSSELS
Many small mussels can become firmly embedded in rock. Here, a natural mineral-cement binds the sediment grains and the fossil shells together, making it difficult for a collector to take the shells out.

FOSSILS WITH COLOR
The shells of living mussels are blue. Some of the color remains in these fossil mussels, which are about two million years old.

LOST COLOR
The color in shells is usually lost during fossilization. The brown color in these fossils is from the rock in which they were fossilized.

The changing world

THE HISTORY OF LIFE has been played out on a world that has been changing constantly since it was formed about 4,600 million years ago (mya). The Earth's crust is divided into several plates which move relative to one another. Most earthquakes and volcanoes occur along boundaries between these plates. The combined effects of many small plate movements have caused continents to drift across the Earth, to collide and form mountains, and to break into pieces. Continents are still moving today. North America is separating from Europe at a rate of about 0.8 in (2 cm) per year. Sea levels and climates have changed many times. This is why fossils of sea creatures can be found inland, and why fossils of tropical plants can be found where the climate is cold. The maps on these pages show the shape of the land at four stages in geological history. The fossils show a selection of the life that existed during each different time span, and many are featured later in this book.

CONTINUOUS CHANGE
Earthquakes such as the great one of Lisbon, Portugal, in 1755 (above), and the one that devastated Armenia, U.S.S.R., in 1988 show that changes are still taking place on Earth.

THE OLDEST FOSSILS
The world's oldest fossils are tiny bacteria-like cells 3,500 million years old. Complex animals made of many cells, like this *Tribrachidium* from Australia, appeared at the end of the Precambrian.

Carboniferous mollusk (bellerophontid)

Carboniferous coral

Silurian trilobites

Silurian graptolites

Devonian fish

Carboniferous seed fern

Silurian brachiopods

Carboniferous crinoid

Silurian gastropod

Gondwanaland

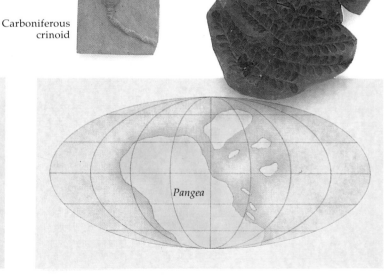

Pangea

EARLY PALEOZOIC WORLD (409–590 MYA)
Paleozoic means "ancient life." During the early Paleozoic Era (Cambrian, Ordovician, and Silurian Periods, p. 9), a large continent, known as Gondwanaland, was situated over the southern polar region. Most early Paleozoic life was in the sea. Invertebrates (animals without backbones) were especially numerous, but primitive fishes were also present. Plants began to live on land toward the end of this time.

LATE PALEOZOIC WORLD (249–408 MYA)
Life diversified greatly during the late Paleozoic Era (Devonian, Carboniferous, and Permian Periods), at the end of which most of the land was joined in one supercontinent known as Pangea. Amphibians, reptiles, insects, and other animals colonized the land where they could feed on the vegetation that had developed. A mass extinction of much of the life occurred at the very end of the Paleozoic.

Skull of Pleistocene
Homo erectus

Toe bone of
Cretaceous
dinosaur

Cretaceous
dinosaur

Skull of Oligocene
mammal

Oligocene
mammal

Skull of Jurassic
ichthyosaur

Jurassic
ichthyosaur

Head of
Triassic amphibian

Oligocene fish

Claw of
Cretaceous
dinosaur

Tooth of
Eocene
shark

Eocene
gastropod

Twig of
Jurassic conifer

Pliocene
bivalve

Eocene
angiosperm

Jurassic
ammonite

Eocene
echinoid

Cretaceous belemnite

Jurassic
bivalve

Pangea

North America

Europe   Asia

Africa

South America

Australasia

MESOZOIC WORLD (66–248 MYA)
Mesozoic means "middle life." The Mesozoic Era (Cretaceous, Jurassic, and Triassic periods) is known as the Age of Reptiles. Dinosaurs stalked the land, pterosaurs swooped through the sky, and ichthyosaurs swam in the sea with belemnites and ammonites. Flowering plants and small mammals appeared, Pangea began to break up, and many species were wiped out in another mass extinction at the end of the Mesozoic.

CENOZOIC WORLD (PRESENT DAY–65 MYA)
The world as we know it gradually took shape during the Cenozoic Era (Paleocene to Holocene epochs). Cenozoic means "recent life." India moved northward and collided with Asia, forming the Himalayas. Mammals and flowering plants became more varied and dominant on land; teleosts (a group of bony fishes) and sea urchins were among groups abundant in the sea. Our own genus, *Homo*, appeared in the Pleistocene.

Early paleontology

THE SERIOUS SCIENTIFIC STUDY OF FOSSILS began only about 300 years ago, although early Greek philosophers such as Pythagoras are reported to have realized the true nature of fossils as long ago as the 5th century B.C. During the Middle Ages in Europe (A.D. 400-1400), many naturalists thought fossils were the products of a mysterious "plastic force" ("*vis plastica*") which formed the fossils within the Earth. Their true origin as the buried remains of ancient animals and plants was established beyond reasonable doubt by Steno (see below) and other naturalists of the 17th century. Fossils were subsequently used to solve geological problems such as the relative ages of different rocks, and also biological problems concerning the evolution and the origin and extinction of various forms of life on Earth. Today scientists throughout the world are still studying fossils, and our understanding of them is increasing all the time.

The frontispiece to the museum catalog of the naturalist Johann Scheuchzer (1672–1733)

TONGUE STONES
Fossil shark teeth from Cenozoic rocks around the Mediterranean were known to naturalists as tongue stones. Some naturalists believed that they grew naturally within the rocks, but Steno and others realized their correct origins.

STENO
Niels Stensen (1638-1686), better known as Steno, was a Dane who worked as the court physician at Florence in Italy. He was one of the first people to realize the true nature of fossils, when in 1667, he noticed that the teeth of a stranded shark were very similar to tongue stones.

NOAH'S ARK
The Bible story of Noah tells how he took animals onto his ark to escape the great flood. Many naturalists, including Steno, believed that the Biblical Flood had transported and buried fossils. This explained why fossil sea shells occurred on mountaintops. (Scheuchzer once identified the fossil of a salamander as the skeleton of a human drowned in the Flood!)

RESTORATION OF PALAEOTHERIUM
Cuvier studied *Palaeotherium* bones from the Eocene rocks of Montmartre in Paris. The animal from which they came was restored as this tapir-like mammal.

Grinding teeth of a herbivore

Fossil jaw of *Palaeotherium*

GEORGES CUVIER
The French naturalist Georges Cuvier (1769–1832) made many important contributions to natural history. Early in his scientific career he realized that the different parts of an animal's body were closely interrelated; for example, mammals with horns and hoofs were all herbivores (plant eaters) and would have had the teeth of herbivores. The significance of this observation was that entire animals could now be restored – shown as they would have looked when alive – from the evidence of isolated bones. Cuvier also recognized that many fossils belonged to extinct species, and he devised a view of Earth history in which a succession of catastrophes exterminated earlier forms of life. According to Cuvier, the last of these catastrophes was the Biblical Flood.

An 18th-century engraving of Harvard University

Upper Carboniferous

Lower Carboniferous

Triassic

Lower Jurassic

Middle Jurassic

LOUIS AGASSIZ

Louis Agassiz (1807–1873) was a Swiss-born naturalist who emigrated to the U.S. where he taught natural history at Harvard University and was one of the first people to encourage an interest in paleontology there. He is especially famous for his detailed studies of fossil fishes. Agassiz was greatly influenced by Cuvier and his catastrophe theories. He re-interpreted some of the youngest rocks, widely believed to be deposits formed by the Biblical Flood, and showed them to have been deposited by glaciers during the Pleistocene Ice Age.

FIRST USEFUL MAP

William Smith, often regarded as the father of English geology, produced the first useful geological maps.

Gastropod

Bivalve hinge

Gastropod

Gastropod

Bivalve

1. *Inoceramus Cuvieri. Thom. Annals V4p.448.*

2. *Inoceramus.*

3. *Cast of the inside of a Trochus.*

4. *Ammonites.*

5. *Pinna depressa. Sowerby M.B.*

6. *Terebratula.*

7. *Terebratula.*

8. *Terebratula subundata. M.C.t.15 f.7.*

9. *Sharks teeth.*

WILLIAM SMITH

The engineer and surveyor William Smith (1769–1839) collected fossils from different rock formations across England. Some of the fossils he collected can be seen here, along with plates from the books in which he illustrated his finds. Smith saw that different layers of rock were characterized by particular species of fossils and realized that rocks containing the same fossil species must be of the same age. Fossils are still used today by geologists to work out the relative ages of rocks, helping them to find oil and other valuable resources.

Gastropod

Ammonite

Fig. 1 *Melania Heddingtonensis. Min. Con. t. 39.*

2 *Turbo ?*

3 *Trochus*

Fig. 5 *Chama*

6 *Ostrea delta. Min. Con. t. 148.*

7 *Ammonites*

Fossil folklore

FOLKLORE IS RICH WITH LEGENDS ABOUT FOSSILS. For at least 10,000 years, fossils have figured in the beliefs and customs of people throughout the world. Even today, many people believe that particular types of fossils have supernatural or medicinal powers. Early people apparently valued particular fossils because of their rarity or natural beauty. The origin of fossils was mysterious to people for a long time and led to some peculiar ideas about them. These ideas were passed down from generation to generation and became part of folklore. We now know what the real origin of fossils is, but it is fascinating to see how our ancestors managed to find an explanation for them.

An artist's idea of the Devil

Carved snake's head

Snakestone (ammonite)

Whitby coat of arms

Ancient Whitby coin

DEVIL'S TOENAIL
The Jurassic oyster *Gryphaea* had a thick curved shell which is still popularly known as a Devil's toenail. This name was given to it in spite of the fact that the Devil has usually been described as having hoofs rather than toes!

SNAKESTONES
Ammonites (pp. 28–29) from Whitby in England were believed to be the remains of coiled snakes turned to stone by the 7th-century abbess St. Hilda. Craftsmen carved heads onto some ammonites to help with this belief. Three snakestones are included in the Whitby coat of arms, seen on this ancient coin.

Thunderstones (fossil sea urchins)

MAGIC STONES
There are many legends about fossil sea urchins (pp. 32–33). Some people thought they were thunderstones which fell from the sky during a thunderstorm. They were believed to keep milk from going sour. One type was thought to be hardened balls of froth made by entwined snakes at midsummer. The snakes tossed them in the air, and if someone caught one in a cloth it had great magical powers (right).

TOADSTONES
The shiny, button-shaped fossil teeth of the Mesozoic fish *Lepidotes* (p. 35) were believed to come from within the heads of toads. This woodcut illustration from 1497 shows the supposed removal of one.

Woodcut of 1497

TOADSTONE MEDICINE
In Europe during the 1400s, toadstones were thought to cure epilepsy and counter poison.

OLD TOAD'S TALE
To be used as medicine, toadstones had to be removed from the head of an old toad while it was alive. Old toads were supposed to eject their stones if they were placed on a red cloth. In reality, toadstones have no connection whatever with toads, but the popular name is still used today for the fossil teeth of the extinct fish, *Lepidotes*.

Toadstones (fossil fish teeth)

FAMOUS MYTH
This illustration showing the mythical unicorn is a detail from a French tapestry called *The Lady and the Unicorn,* dating from about 1500.

Unicornum verum (fossil mammoth tusk)

REAL UNICORN
The tusk of a small whale called the narwhal was for many years identified as the horn of the unicorn. However, the discovery in about 1600 of some fossil mammoth tusks led to *these* being proclaimed as the true horns of unicorns, or *unicornum verum.*

LUCKY SPINES
These are the club-shaped spines of the sea urchin *Balanocidaris.* They can be found in Cretaceous rocks in an area in the Middle East that used to be called Judea hence their name of Jewstones. They were used as good luck charms as long ago as 650 B.C.

Natural hole through sponge

Porosphaera

SPONGE BEADS
Bronze Age people in Britain made necklaces by stringing together certain fossil sponges. Some specimens of the Cretaceous sponge *Porosphaera* are remarkably like beads. Many even have a natural hole through the middle, probably caused by the sponge's having grown around part of another creature or plant.

BRONZE AGE BURIAL
The skeletons of this woman and her child were found buried on Dunstable Down, England. Around the grave were three rows of fossil sea urchins, buried with the woman and child about three thousand years ago, maybe to ward off evil spirits.

Thunderbolts (belemnites)

Stone swallow (fossil brachiopod)

TAKE ONE SHELL
In China the fossil shells of certain brachiopods (p. 25) are called *Shiy-yen* (stone swallows) and are still used as medicine. According to the prescription supplied with these Devonian brachiopods, they should be ground up, baked in a clay pot, and taken as a cure for many illnesses including rheumatism, cataracts, anemia, and digestive problems. The medicine is described as sweet and cooling.

THUNDERBOLTS
These are the internal shells of extinct squidlike animals called belemnites (p. 29). In folklore they were thought to have been flung down as darts from the heavens during thunderstorms, and they supposedly had medicinal powers. Belemnites have also been found with human skeletons in ancient burial mounds.

Fossils of the future

THE FOSSIL RECORD is a highly selective sample of ancient life. Many creatures rotted away entirely because they did not have resistant hard parts. Some lived in environments where burial and fossilization were unlikely to occur; for example, in treetops. Others lived in oceans, lakes, and rivers where fossilization was more likely. Yet, even in these environments, only a small proportion of life would have been fossilized. This selectivity is well illustrated by looking at a modern community to see which animals and plants might become fossils of the future.

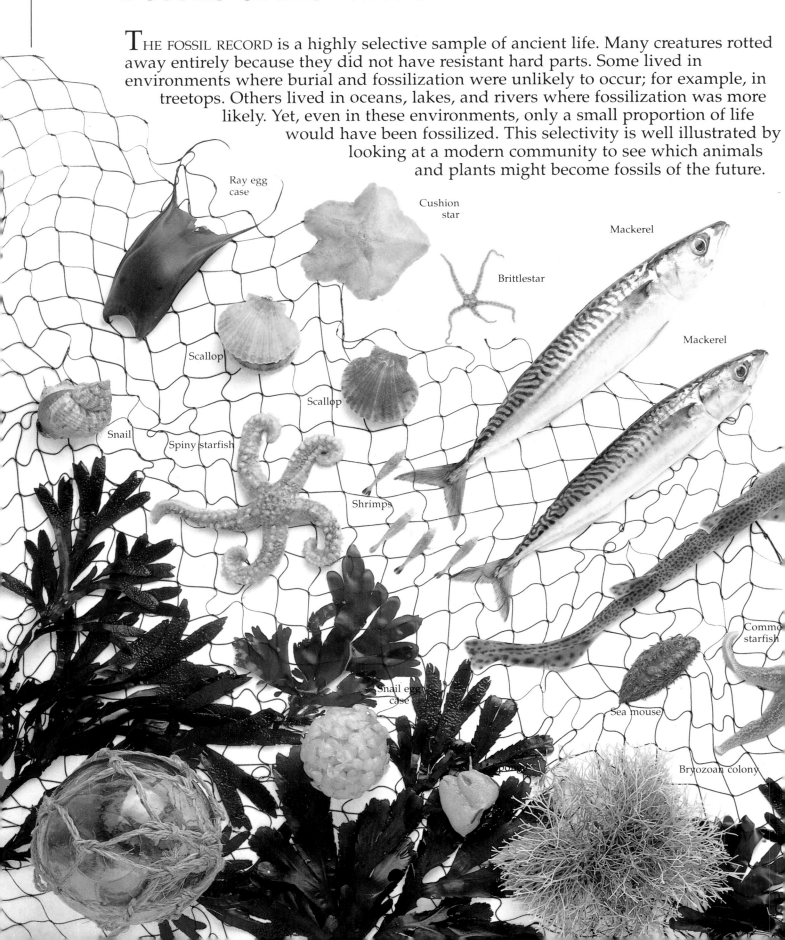

Ray egg case

Cushion star

Brittlestar

Mackerel

Mackerel

Scallop

Scallop

Snail

Spiny starfish

Shrimps

Snail egg case

Common starfish

Sea mouse

Bryozoan colony

TEMPORARY TENANT

A good example of a creature that is unlikely to leave direct evidence of its existence is the hermit crab. Hermit crabs are unusual in having no shell of their own. They use abandoned snail shells as homes. In some habitats every available snail shell contains a hermit crab. Much of a hermit crab's body is soft and it twists in the spiral of the snail shell. The claws are hard but are rarely fossilized and are almost never found within the shell occupied by the crab. This is probably because decay of the organic material in the claws causes them to disintegrate before fossilization. However, when looking at fossil snail shells, it is worth bearing in mind that they may have had two tenants – a snail and a hermit crab.

Mackerel skeletons

Dogfish teeth   Crab shell

Scallop shells

Edible sea urchin skeleton

Green sea urchin skeleton

Snail shell

Dogfish

THE SAMPLE

Water communities are common in the fossil record because creatures that live in oceans, lakes, and rivers are liable to be buried by the mud or sand which is often deposited in these environments. Most of this sample of animals and plants lived on the sea bed; the fishes and shrimps swam in the waters above. Among the other animals present are sea urchins, starfishes, a brittlestar, scallops, a snail, a small crab, a sponge, a sea mouse (worm), and bryozoan and hydroid colonies. Note also the egg cases of a snail, a dogfish, and a ray. The seaweeds are brown algae of the sort which grow in great quantities along the shoreline.

Common starfish skeleton

Cushion star skeleton

Spiny starfish skeleton

THE REMAINS

The parts of animals that are most likely to be fossilized are the hard parts such as teeth, bones, and shells. The hard parts of the sample of animals and plants are shown together here. The seaweeds and many of the animals have disappeared entirely. Others have left very little trace. All that remains of the dogfish, for example, are its teeth. A dogfish has a skeleton of nonresistant cartilage, not bone. The sea urchins, starfishes, brittlestar, crab, and bryozoans had resistant skeletons. However, these consisted of many separate pieces which have now mostly fallen apart as the soft tissues connecting them decayed. Only the snail and scallop shells have survived with little obvious change. The mackerel bones and crab shell would probably decay before fossilization unless buried very rapidly because they contain a lot of organic material. This illustrates dramatically how little of a modern community would usually survive to be fossilized. The same was true for communities of the geological past.

Brittlestar skeleton

Bryozoan skeletons

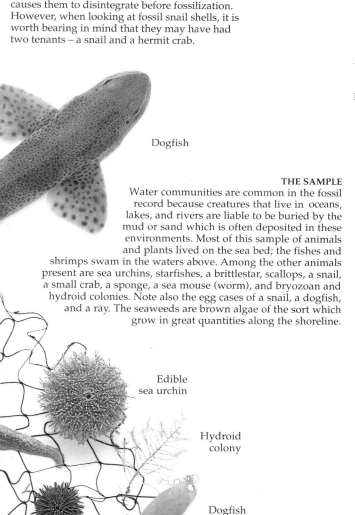

Edible sea urchin

Hydroid colony

Dogfish egg case

Green sea urchin

crab

LEAVING NO TRACE

Animals and plants living and dying on land often decay completely before they can be buried and fossilized. The fur and flesh of this reindeer carcass, photographed in the Arctic, are beginning to rot away from the bones. These too will disintegrate unless by chance they are buried.

Remarkable remains

Skin traces

Part   **IN TWO PARTS**   Counterpart

The outline of the body is clearly shown in this fossilized frog. Even traces of the skin and other fleshy tissues have been preserved. The rock has split straight through the preserved animal, leaving the fossil in two pieces known as the part and counterpart.

FOSSILS OF SOFT TISSUES, which usually decay during fossilization, are sometimes found. These include entirely soft-bodied animals which are otherwise unrepresented in the fossil record. Fossilization of soft parts is of great importance because it supplies much more information about the living animals than do bones, teeth, or shells. Discoveries of preserved humans are always exciting and include those at Pompeii in Italy and Grauballe in Denmark.

STICKY DEATH

A spider can clearly be seen in this piece of amber, the fossilized resin of an ancient plant. Amber often contains animals that were trapped in the sticky resin as it dripped down trunks and stems. Insects, spiders, and even small lizards and frogs have been preserved for millions of years in this way.

UNIQUE INFORMATION

This unusual worm is from a deposit known as the Burgess Shale in British Columbia, Canada, famous for its soft-bodied fossils. Other animals discovered in the Burgess Shale include trilobites (p. 30) with their limbs intact, primitive crustaceans, and several bizarre creatures that do not fit within any groups living today. These animals were buried in mudflows on the Cambrian sea bed over 500 million years ago, and their fossils provide us with a unique glimpse of a very varied early community.

EXCEPTIONAL INSECT

This delicate dragonfly was buried in mud which formed the Solnhofen Limestone of Bavaria, West Germany, a deposit renowned for its exceptional fossils.

DEEP-FROZEN MAMMOTH

Mammoths have occasionally been recovered from the permafrost (permanently frozen ground) of Siberia, northern Asia. They were probably trapped and frozen when they fell into cracks in glaciers. Mammoths lived during the Ice Ages of the last two million years and became extinct about 12,000 years ago. The largest species grew to over 13 ft (4 m) at the shoulder.

ACTIVE VOLCANO

The famous volcano Vesuvius in southeast Italy has erupted frequently over the years. It has been quiet since 1944 but is not thought to be extinct.

Cast of body from Pompeii

BURIED IN ASH

During the violent eruption of Mount Vesuvius in A.D. 79, inhabitants of the nearby towns of Pompeii and Herculaneum were buried beneath avalanches of volcanic ash and debris. The bodies lasted long enough for the ash to harden around them, and when they decayed they left cavities. The cavities were excavated and then filled with plaster to make casts, which gruesomely revealed victims' postures at the moment of death. Some bodies of pets have also been found.

SOFT PRESERVATION *left*
Belemnoteuthis from the Jurassic is related to squid, cuttlefish, and the extinct belemnites (p. 29). The internal skeleton of this specimen is hidden beneath the soft body, which has been preserved because of replacement by the mineral apatite soon after death and burial. Even the hooked tentacles around the head can be seen. Ink was released from a sac as a defensive screen, an ability that *Belemnoteuthis's* relatives possess today.

Hooked tentacles

Preserved soft body hides the internal skeleton

The cast of the body shows exactly how this person was lying when buried by ash over 1,900 years ago

Bone

Skin

Fossil moa foot

Claw

SKINNY CLAW
The moas of New Zealand were large flightless birds related to the kiwi, emu, and ostrich. The biggest was 11 ft (3.5 m) tall. Although now extinct, moas were alive when Maoris first lived in New Zealand 700 years ago. Fossils of many different species of moa have been found, some over two million years old. This fossilized foot still has skin attached. The impact these once dominant birds had on New Zealand's native vegetation is still evident today in plants that have evolved a resistance to being eaten by moas!

A moa among kiwis

Reconstruction of a mammoth stuck in the tar at La Brea

STUCK FAST
Tar oozing naturally to the surface at La Brea in Los Angeles, California, has entombed many animals accidentally caught in the sticky substance over the past 10,000 to 20,000 years. Excavations in the older solidified layers of tar have unearthed the bones of extinct mammals such as mammoths and saber-toothed cats (p. 55).

GRAUBALLE MAN
Human bodies in remarkable states of preservation have been excavated from several peat bogs in northern Europe. The acid material of the bogs prevented the total decay of soft parts. Many bodies are over 2,000 years old, and some show signs of a ritual killing. This man was found in 1952 near the village of Grauballe in Denmark. He died in about the 4th century. Skin and internal organs – even re-mains of his last meal – have been preserved.

Corals

CORALS ARE SOME OF THE MOST BEAUTIFUL ANIMALS in the sea. The colorful massed tentacles of coral individuals, or polyps, resemble flowers in an undersea garden. Most corals live in warm, shallow, tropical waters and feed on plankton but also obtain nutrition from algae which may live within their bodies. Corals may be solitary (living by themselves) or colonial (many polyps joined together). Fossil corals are common because beneath the soft-bodied polyps are hard, chalky skeletons. The oldest are from the Ordovician. Related sea anemones and jellyfish lack hard skeletons and are seldom fossilized.

CORAL FISHING
Coral has long been collected for its beauty and is used in jewelry.

A ring-shaped coral reef is called an atoll

Separate corallite

Individual coral skeleton

Red limestone

PIPE CORAL
This is a colony of *Acrocyathus*, a Carboniferous coral. The pipe-shaped corallites (skeletons formed by individual polyps) grew separately. The spaces between them are now filled with red limestone.

HORN CORAL
Aulophyllum, shown here in two pieces, is a typical solitary coral. It lived on the sea bed, growing in this characteristic horn shape. The pointed end was buried in sediment on the sea bed, and the soft polyp sat on top of the other end.

PACKED COLONY
Lonsdaleia is a colonial coral which belongs to a group called the Rugosa. Rugose corals became extinct in the Permian. The individual corallites which make up the colony are many-sided, usually hexagonal (six-sided), because they are so tightly packed together.

MODERN CORALS
Most modern corals belong to a group called the scleractinians which first appeared in the Triassic. Coral reefs are inhabited by countless numbers of different animals and are the most diverse marine environments.

CHAIN CORAL
The corallites of the Silurian coral *Halysites* are arranged in long branching ribbons. On the surface, the coral looks like a collection of chains.

Pale sediment filling areas once occupied by soft tissues

Branch of corallites

BRAIN CORAL
Together, the individuals of brain corals form winding valleys, and the colonies resemble human brains. Polyps may share a common mouth with others in the same valley. This Miocene example has been cut horizontally and polished to show the inside.

Winding valley of coral

RECORD-BREAKING CORAL
This fossilized fragment is of the reef-building coral *Galaxea*. The structure of the individual skeletons can easily be seen. The world's largest known living coral is a *Galaxea* colony from Okinawa in Japan. It has a circumference (outer boundary) of 52 ft (16 m).

Individual coral skeleton

CORAL BUSH
Colonies of the coral *Thamnopora* are bush-shaped, with corallites opening all over the surfaces of the branches. This example is in a piece of limestone which has been cut across horizontally and polished to show the shape of the colony.

Fossil *Fungia*

SOLITARY CORALS
These unusual-looking fossils are the delicate skeletons of the solitary corals *Stephanophyllia* and *Fungia*, which lived on the sea bed in the Pliocene and Pleistocene respectively. As their name suggests, the skeletons of *Fungia* look like the undersides of mushrooms.

REPLACED CORAL
The skeletons of some fossil corals are made of the mineral aragonite. Aragonite dissolves easily, so the skeletons often disappear during fossilization. In this fossil colony of *Thecosmilia* the skeletons have been replaced by silica.

Skeleton replaced by silica

Fossil *Stephanophyllia*

Sea bed dwellers

CLOSE NEIGHBORS
Bryozoan colonies can be compared to blocks of apartments and other buildings containing several similar homes.

AMONG THE MOST COMMON FOSSILS to be found are the remains of animals and plants which lived on the sea bed. They lived where sand and mud were regularly deposited, and most of the animals had hard parts which could survive decay and be fossilized. The plants and many of the animals could not escape burial, even when they were alive, because they lacked the ability to move. Bryozoans and brachiopods are living examples of this type of animal but because they live in the sea, many people are not aware of their existence. Today, there are only 250 known species of brachiopods. This contrasts with the huge numbers – about 30,000 – of known fossil species.

Holes in the colony through which water and food particles are pumped

ARCHIMEDES' SCREW
This distinctive Carboniferous bryozoan is named after a spiral water pump invented by the Greek mathematician Archimedes. The screw-shaped skeleton once supported a twisted net of individuals similar to *Hornera* (center left).

Archimedes' water pump

COMMUNITY HOMES *above*
Because of their branching shape, this type of modern bryozoan, *Hornera*, often provides a home for worms, small fishes, and many other animals in the sea.

One individual skeleton

Each piece is a colony containing at least 200 individuals

LARGER THAN LIFE
The calcite skeletons of individuals in a bryozoan colony are magnified here many times.

Free-living colonies of Cretaceous bryozoans

Light and dark growth bands

Calcite colonies

Bryozoans are tiny animals which live in colonies where each individual is attached to its neighbor. A colony may contain tens, hundreds, or even thousands of individuals, each one less than 0.04 in (1 mm) long. They have tentacles which they use to feed on tiny particles of food. Most have calcite skeletons. Colonies, which grow by budding new individuals, vary in shape. Some are flat sheets; others grow upright and look like nets or bushes.

BEETROOT STONE
The red color of the Jurassic alga *Solenopora* is sometimes preserved, and these fossils are then known as beetroot stones.

OLD LACE
The fragments of lace bryozoan (*Chasmatopora*) in this Ordovician shale are among the oldest known bryozoans.

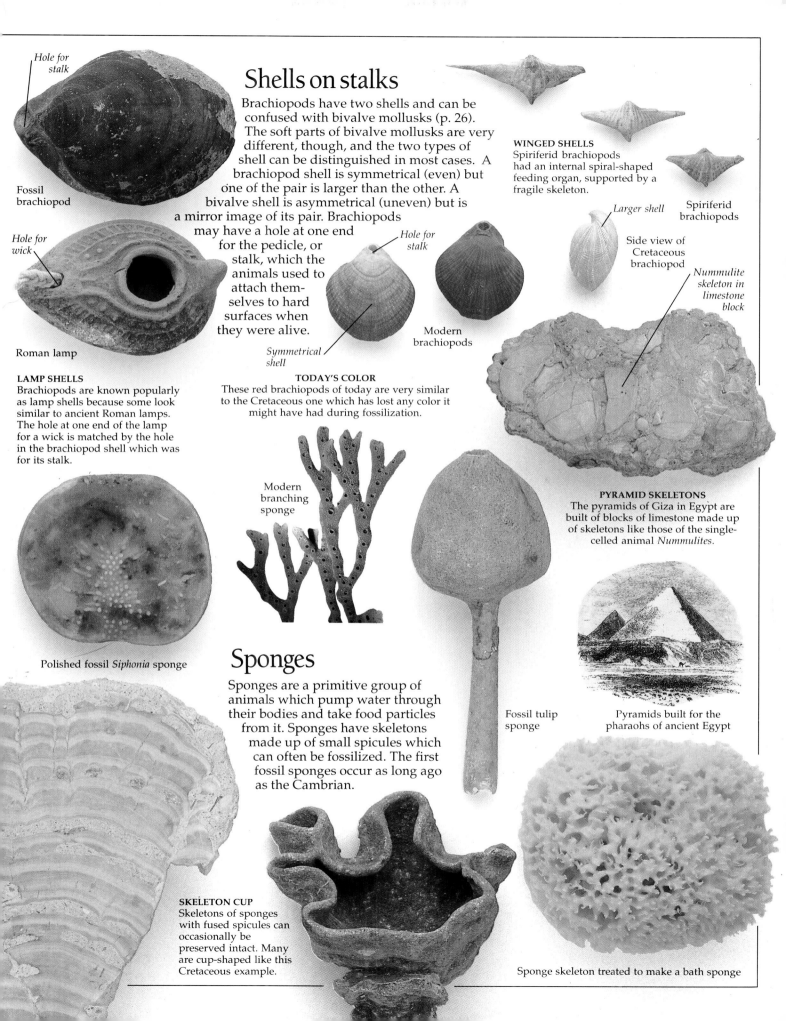

Hole for stalk

Fossil brachiopod

Hole for wick

Roman lamp

Shells on stalks

Brachiopods have two shells and can be confused with bivalve mollusks (p. 26). The soft parts of bivalve mollusks are very different, though, and the two types of shell can be distinguished in most cases. A brachiopod shell is symmetrical (even) but one of the pair is larger than the other. A bivalve shell is asymmetrical (uneven) but is a mirror image of its pair. Brachiopods may have a hole at one end for the pedicle, or stalk, which the animals used to attach themselves to hard surfaces when they were alive.

WINGED SHELLS
Spiriferid brachiopods had an internal spiral-shaped feeding organ, supported by a fragile skeleton.

Larger shell

Spiriferid brachiopods

Side view of Cretaceous brachiopod

Nummulite skeleton in limestone block

Hole for stalk

Symmetrical shell

Modern brachiopods

LAMP SHELLS
Brachiopods are known popularly as lamp shells because some look similar to ancient Roman lamps. The hole at one end of the lamp for a wick is matched by the hole in the brachiopod shell which was for its stalk.

TODAY'S COLOR
These red brachiopods of today are very similar to the Cretaceous one which has lost any color it might have had during fossilization.

Modern branching sponge

Polished fossil *Siphonia* sponge

Sponges

Sponges are a primitive group of animals which pump water through their bodies and take food particles from it. Sponges have skeletons made up of small spicules which can often be fossilized. The first fossil sponges occur as long ago as the Cambrian.

PYRAMID SKELETONS
The pyramids of Giza in Egypt are built of blocks of limestone made up of skeletons like those of the single-celled animal *Nummulites*.

Fossil tulip sponge

Pyramids built for the pharaohs of ancient Egypt

SKELETON CUP
Skeletons of sponges with fused spicules can occasionally be preserved intact. Many are cup-shaped like this Cretaceous example.

Sponge skeleton treated to make a bath sponge

Shells of all shapes

AT THE BEGINNING of the Cambrian period, about 550 million years ago, complex animals with hard shells and skeletons first appeared in the sea. Among these were the mollusks, a group of animals which are still abundant today. Gastropods, or snails, and bivalves such as clams, mussels, and oysters, are the best-known mollusks; other kinds include chitons and cephalopods (p. 29). Bivalves have two shells, or valves, joined together by a hinge. Gastropods have only one shell. The shells of mollusks are often found as fossils. Most are made of calcite, or of aragonite which dissolves more easily. Internal molds of mollusks are often found because aragonite shells may become filled with sediment and the shells themselves dissolved.

VENUS'S SHELL
The Roman goddess Venus emerging from a scallop shell.

Pearl

ANCIENT JEWELS
This mudstone contains rare fossil pearls. They are from the Eocene, and are about 50 million years old.

Hinge tooth

Muscle scar

HINGED TOGETHER
Hinge teeth help hold a bivalve's shells together when it is alive. This shell belonged to an Eocene bivalve, *Venericardia*.

Shell   *Eye*

Gape

Sensory tentacles

GOOD EYESIGHT
Scallops have many eyes, each of which has well-developed focusing lenses. The eyes are situated in soft tissue near the edge of the shells, which are hinged together. To feed, scallops open their shells and use their gills to force a current of water, laden with food particles, through the "gape" in the shells.

SPINES FOR SPONGES
The "thorny oyster" *Spondylus* is so named because of its spiny shell, as seen in this Pliocene specimen. Spines of modern *Spondylus* help sponges and other encrusting animals grow on their shells, which protects the bivalve from predators.

Prominent rib

FALLING APART
These fossilized shells, one flat, the other convex (domed), belong to the scallop *Pecten* from the Pliocene. The prominent ribs on the two shells interlock, but, as with many bivalve fossils, the shells are usually found separated because the connecting ligament rots away.

CARVED IN STONE
An ancient Arabic prayer has been carved on these two fossils. They are internal casts (p. 6) of bivalves, formed by sediment which solidified in the space between the shells.

Modern Cone
shell

Fossil Cone
shell

Modern snail shell

Fossil snail shells

DISAPPEARING COLOR
Some living gastropods, especially those of the tropics, are often brightly colored because of chemical substances within the shell called pigments. Unfortunately, pigments are usually destroyed during fossilization.

— *Siphon*

— *Foot*

SOFT-HEARTED
This present-day sea snail is just emerging from its shell. Parts of its soft body can clearly be seen (at top and bottom right).

Modern snail

Curious coils

Gastropod shells of all ages come in many different shapes and sizes. They are all open at one end and are usually twisted into a spiral coil with a gradually increasing diameter. The exact shape of the spiral varies according to the species. It can be left-handed, right-handed, loosely coiled or tightly coiled, regular or irregular. The coiling of the shell on the freshwater snail *Planorbis* is almost flat. The shell of *Turritella* is drawn out into a high spire.

Spiral coil

Fossil
Turritella

"WORM SHELLS"
Vermetids are unusual for gastropods as they attach themselves permanently to a hard surface, often in clusters like these fossil examples. Their shells are irregularly coiled and look more like worms.

Fossil chiton

Modern
chiton

NO CONNECTION
Chitons are a small group of marine mollusks with shells made up of eight individual plates. Fossil chitons are rare and their plates are disconnected. Today, chitons can be found in tide pools, clinging to the sides of the rocks from which they scrape algae for food.

LOOSE COILS
Tubina is a very unusual type of mollusk which belonged to a now-extinct group called the bellerophontids. It has a loosely coiled shell and dates from the Devonian Period. It is uncertain whether *Tubina* was a true gastropod or not because its soft body has not been preserved.

Left-handed coil

Right-handed coil

SPIRAL FOSSILS
Most gastropod shells have a right-handed spiral coil, such as *Neptunea despecta*. The shell of *Neptunea contraria* has a left-handed coil.

Fossil *Neptunea contraria*

Fossil *Neptunea despecta*

— *Siphonal canal*

EXTRA LONG
The pointed shell of *Fusinus* is further lengthened by a siphonal canal which the animal used in respiration.

Top

Fossil *Planorbis*

Underneath

Intelligent mollusks

An ammonite with its shell partly replaced by iron pyrites

DECORATIVE MOTIF
The beautiful shape of ammonites is often used in decoration. This is a column from a terraced house in Brighton, England. The architect's name was Amon!

THE OCTOPUS, SQUID, and cuttlefish are modern representatives of a group of sea-dwelling mollusks called cephalopods, which have left a rich fossil record. Cephalopods are regarded as the most highly developed mollusks. They have suckered tentacles, eyes that are remarkably similar to more advanced vertebrate animals, and the ability to learn and use their learning. They are active predators, moving quickly through the water using a type of jet propulsion. Most modern cephalopods have internal shells completely covered by soft parts. However, like the living *Nautilus*, many fossil cephalopods, including the ammonites, had external shells that were similar to the shells of snails but were divided into chambers. Following their first appearance in the Cambrian, many different species of cephalopods came and went, making them very useful fossils for dating rocks (p. 9).

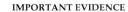

IMPORTANT EVIDENCE
As the only living nautiloid, *Nautilus* is the closest modern relative of the ammonites, and provides us with important clues about this extinct group. *Nautilus* is a nocturnal animal, active only at night, and lives in the Pacific Ocean at depths ranging from 16 to 1,800 ft (5 to 550 m). Its prey consists of fish and crustaceans which it eats with its hard beak.

Septa dividing shell into chambers

Final chamber

Complex suture line

Ammonites

VARIOUS SIZES
Some Mesozoic ammonites reached gigantic sizes. This large specimen, about 12 in (30 cm) wide, is small compared to giants which could be 6 ft (2 m) in diameter.

Simple suture line

Fossil nautiloids

ROOMS FOR EXPANSION
Fossil ammonites and nautiloids have coiled shells divided into a series of chambers by membranes called septa. Only the final chamber next to the opening was occupied by the animal. As it grew, the animal periodically moved forward and formed new septa at the rear of the body chamber. Older chambers were filled with liquid and gas, the proportions of which could be changed through a canal called the siphuncle to allow the animal to move up and down in the sea. Suture lines, formed where the septa meet the shell, are simple in nautiloids but are folded into complex saddles and lobes in ammonites.

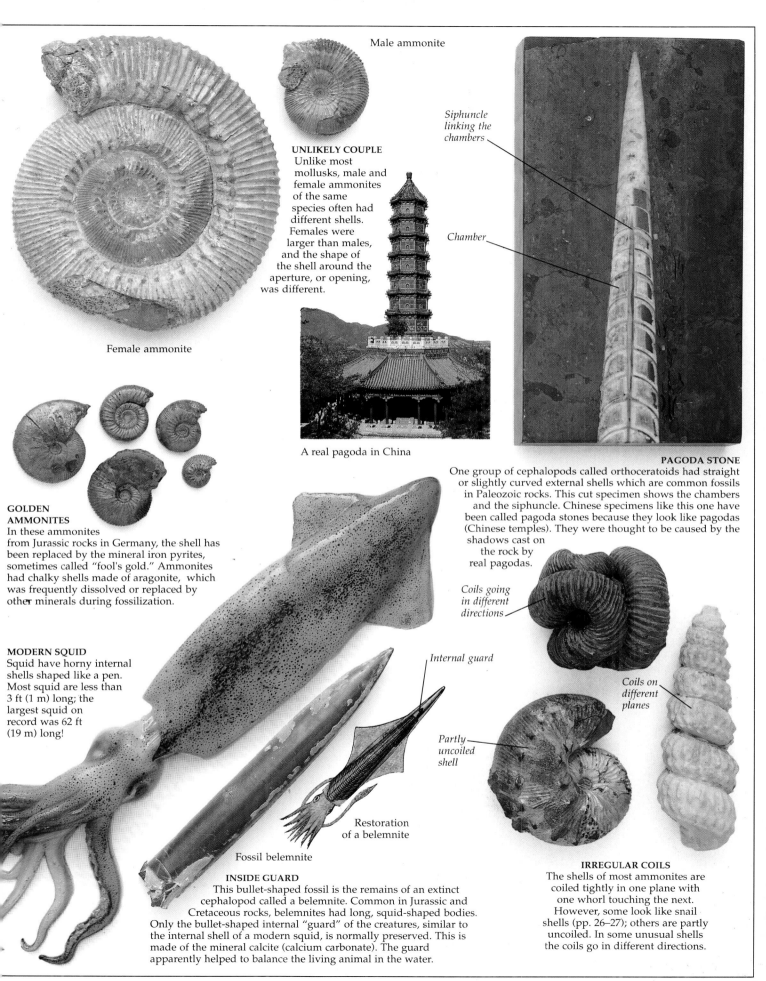

Male ammonite

UNLIKELY COUPLE
Unlike most mollusks, male and female ammonites of the same species often had different shells. Females were larger than males, and the shape of the shell around the aperture, or opening, was different.

Female ammonite

A real pagoda in China

Siphuncle linking the chambers

Chamber

PAGODA STONE
One group of cephalopods called orthoceratoids had straight or slightly curved external shells which are common fossils in Paleozoic rocks. This cut specimen shows the chambers and the siphuncle. Chinese specimens like this one have been called pagoda stones because they look like pagodas (Chinese temples). They were thought to be caused by the shadows cast on the rock by real pagodas.

GOLDEN AMMONITES
In these ammonites from Jurassic rocks in Germany, the shell has been replaced by the mineral iron pyrites, sometimes called "fool's gold." Ammonites had chalky shells made of aragonite, which was frequently dissolved or replaced by other minerals during fossilization.

MODERN SQUID
Squid have horny internal shells shaped like a pen. Most squid are less than 3 ft (1 m) long; the largest squid on record was 62 ft (19 m) long!

Internal guard

Coils going in different directions

Partly uncoiled shell

Coils on different planes

Restoration of a belemnite

Fossil belemnite

INSIDE GUARD
This bullet-shaped fossil is the remains of an extinct cephalopod called a belemnite. Common in Jurassic and Cretaceous rocks, belemnites had long, squid-shaped bodies. Only the bullet-shaped internal "guard" of the creatures, similar to the internal shell of a modern squid, is normally preserved. This is made of the mineral calcite (calcium carbonate). The guard apparently helped to balance the living animal in the water.

IRREGULAR COILS
The shells of most ammonites are coiled tightly in one plane with one whorl touching the next. However, some look like snail shells (pp. 26–27); others are partly uncoiled. In some unusual shells the coils go in different directions.

Animals in armor

Insects, spiders, crabs, scorpions, lobsters, millipedes, barnacles, and many other animals belong to a major group of animals called arthropods, a word which means "jointed foot." Some arthropods live in the sea, some live on land, and some fly; but very few are found as fossils. All arthropods have jointed legs, a segmented body, and an exoskeleton, or outer armor. As the animal grows, it has to shed its exoskeleton every so often and grow another one. Some arthropods – the extinct trilobites, for example – have the mineral calcite in their exoskeletons, making them resistant to decay. These exoskeletons are the parts of arthropods most commonly found fossilized.

PRIZE POSSESSION
Trilobites are prized fossils. This Silurian *Calymene* has been made into a brooch. Examples of this species were found in such great numbers at Dudley, England, that they were nicknamed Dudley bugs.

SMALL IS BEAUTIFUL
Most trilobites were 1 to 4 in (3 to 10 cm) long. These are examples of *Elrathia*.

No eyes

Eyes

TO SEE OR NOT TO SEE?
There were more than 10,000 different species of trilobites and all of them lived in the sea. Some crawled along the sea bed, others floated or swam through the water. Most species had two eyes and could probably see very well. Lenses are sometimes preserved in fossil trilobites because they were made of the mineral calcite. Some species, however, were eyeless. Most of these lived in darkness in the deep sea, beyond the depth to which natural light penetrates.

Modern millipede

Fossil millipede

EARLY SETTLERS
Like all arthropods, millipedes have bodies divided into segments, or sections. Unlike the other arthropods on these pages, they live on land and were among the first animals to do so. Fossil millipedes are seldom found.

Trilobite *Dalmanites*

Trilobite *Concoryphe*

Packed lenses

MULTIVISION
Trilobite eyes are the most ancient visual systems known. They consisted of many separate lenses packed together. Each lens produced its own image.

Echinocaris, a Devonian shrimplike arthropod

ROLL UP!
Some trilobites were able to roll up like wood lice, probably for protection against predators.

Long spine

TRI-LOBED
The name trilobite was given to these creatures because their exoskeletons are divided into three distinct lobes, or parts. The soft parts and the legs on the lower surface of the animal were very seldom preserved. Whole fossil trilobites are surprisingly rare, but they can be found in rocks from the Cambrian to the Permian Period (about 590 to 250 million years old). They became extinct after that. This one is *Paradoxides* from the Cambrian. One of the biggest of all trilobites, it grew to 1 ft 7 in (50 cm) long.

PRICKLY CUSTOMER
This Devonian trilobite, *Dicranurus*, was notable for its long spines, which are superbly preserved in this specimen.

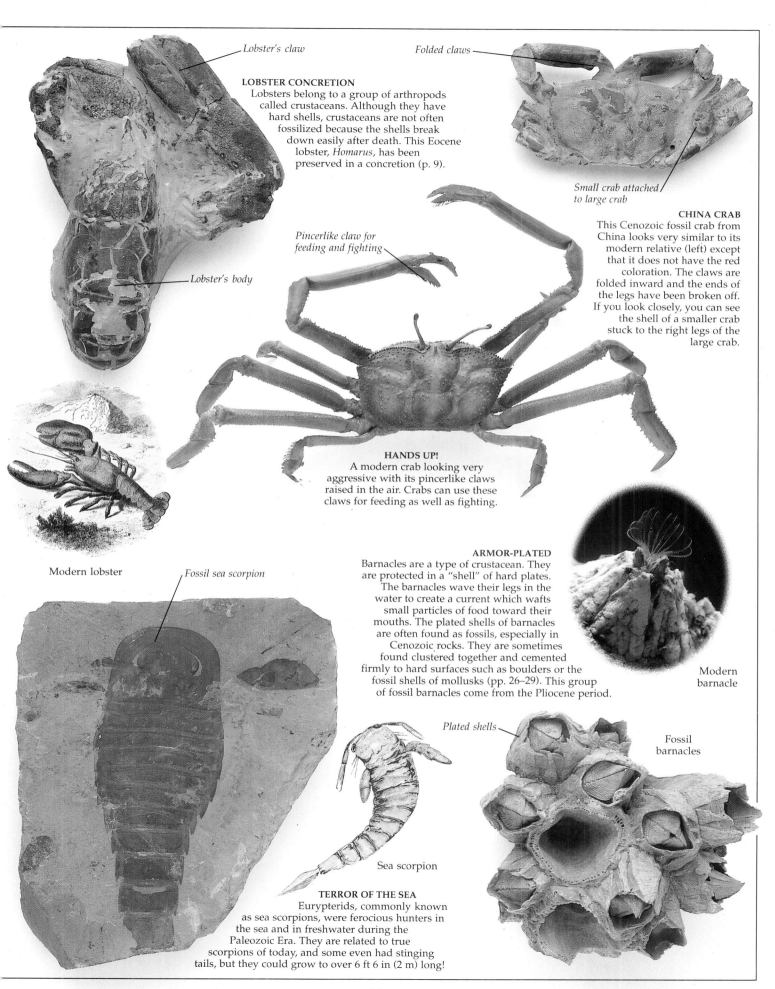

LOBSTER CONCRETION
Lobsters belong to a group of arthropods called crustaceans. Although they have hard shells, crustaceans are not often fossilized because the shells break down easily after death. This Eocene lobster, *Homarus*, has been preserved in a concretion (p. 9).

Lobster's claw

Folded claws

Small crab attached to large crab

CHINA CRAB
This Cenozoic fossil crab from China looks very similar to its modern relative (left) except that it does not have the red coloration. The claws are folded inward and the ends of the legs have been broken off. If you look closely, you can see the shell of a smaller crab stuck to the right legs of the large crab.

Pincerlike claw for feeding and fighting

Lobster's body

HANDS UP!
A modern crab looking very aggressive with its pincerlike claws raised in the air. Crabs can use these claws for feeding as well as fighting.

Modern lobster

Fossil sea scorpion

ARMOR-PLATED
Barnacles are a type of crustacean. They are protected in a "shell" of hard plates. The barnacles wave their legs in the water to create a current which wafts small particles of food toward their mouths. The plated shells of barnacles are often found as fossils, especially in Cenozoic rocks. They are sometimes found clustered together and cemented firmly to hard surfaces such as boulders or the fossil shells of mollusks (pp. 26–29). This group of fossil barnacles come from the Pliocene period.

Modern barnacle

Plated shells

Fossil barnacles

Sea scorpion

TERROR OF THE SEA
Eurypterids, commonly known as sea scorpions, were ferocious hunters in the sea and in freshwater during the Paleozoic Era. They are related to true scorpions of today, and some even had stinging tails, but they could grow to over 6 ft 6 in (2 m) long!

Arms and spines

ECHINODERMS are a very distinctive group of animals which all live in the sea. Among them are sea urchins (echinoids), sea lilies (crinoids), starfish (asteroids), and brittlestars (ophiuroids). The distinguishing feature of most echinoderms is their fivefold radial symmetry. That is, their bodies can be divided into five similar segments, kind of like the segments of an orange. As echinoderms have skeletons made of calcite, they are often found fossilized. Indeed, fossil echinoderms range back to the Cambrian. Echinoderm skeletons consist of many individual pieces or plates, each grown as a single crystal of calcite. These are often separated and scattered soon after the animal dies, so rapid burial is especially important to ensure good preservation.

Modern brittlestar

Delicate interlinked arms

BURIED ALIVE
This exceptional Jurassic specimen shows a group of five fossil brittlestars with arms interlinked. These may have been buried while still alive, as the plated skeletons are normally scattered soon after death. Brittlestars look like starfish but are more delicate and their arms break off easily, hence their name. They use their arms to move across the sea bed. Some feed on plankton; others are scavengers.

Symmetrical arm

STAR HUNTER
Many starfish are very efficient hunters, often feeding on clams and oysters which they open using the suckers on their arms. Others, like this Australian *Protoreaster*, extract their food from sediments such as sand.

Modern *Protoreaster*

STAR OF THE BEACH
Starfish are familiar to anyone who has explored tide pools and beaches by the sea, but they are very seldom found as fossils.

Mouth

Suckers

Mouth

Underside of modern starfish

Position of missing arm

Ammonite

ARM ROBBERY
This fossil starfish from the Jurassic, seen from underneath, is remarkably similar to some present-day species but unfortunately one of its arms is missing. Its mouth can be seen in the center. The rock in which it is embedded contains small ammonites and many shell fragments as well.

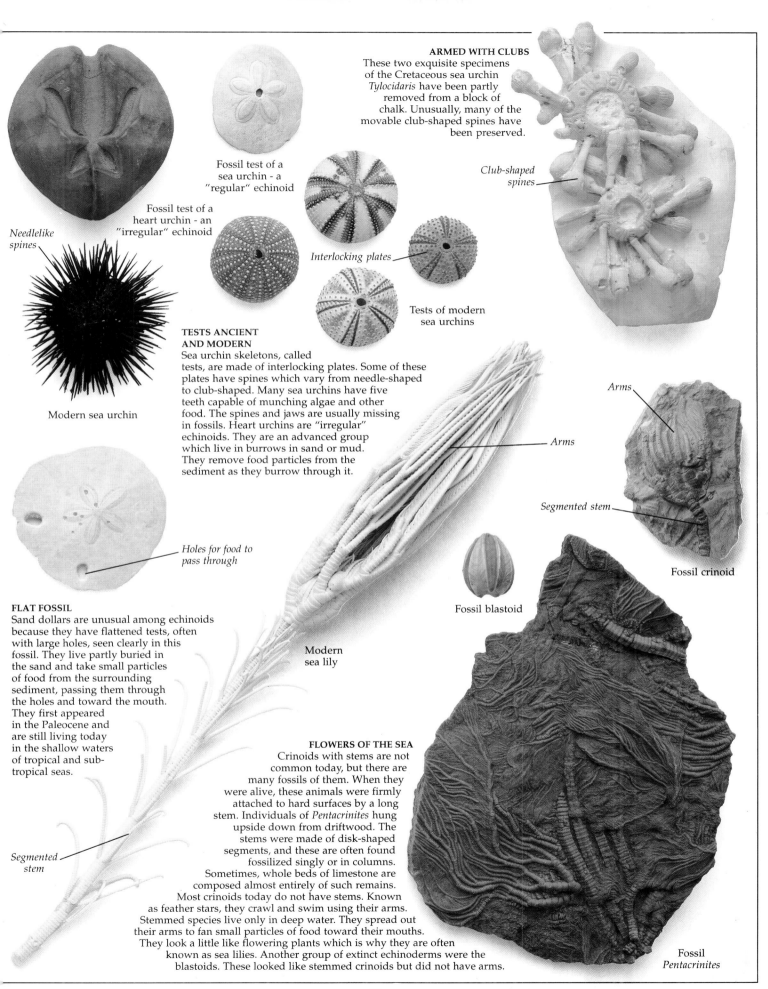

ARMED WITH CLUBS
These two exquisite specimens of the Cretaceous sea urchin *Tylocidaris* have been partly removed from a block of chalk. Unusually, many of the movable club-shaped spines have been preserved.

Club-shaped spines

Fossil test of a sea urchin - a "regular" echinoid

Fossil test of a heart urchin - an "irregular" echinoid

Interlocking plates

Tests of modern sea urchins

Needlelike spines

Modern sea urchin

TESTS ANCIENT AND MODERN
Sea urchin skeletons, called tests, are made of interlocking plates. Some of these plates have spines which vary from needle-shaped to club-shaped. Many sea urchins have five teeth capable of munching algae and other food. The spines and jaws are usually missing in fossils. Heart urchins are "irregular" echinoids. They are an advanced group which live in burrows in sand or mud. They remove food particles from the sediment as they burrow through it.

Arms

Arms

Segmented stem

Fossil crinoid

Holes for food to pass through

Modern sea lily

Fossil blastoid

FLAT FOSSIL
Sand dollars are unusual among echinoids because they have flattened tests, often with large holes, seen clearly in this fossil. They live partly buried in the sand and take small particles of food from the surrounding sediment, passing them through the holes and toward the mouth. They first appeared in the Paleocene and are still living today in the shallow waters of tropical and sub-tropical seas.

Segmented stem

FLOWERS OF THE SEA
Crinoids with stems are not common today, but there are many fossils of them. When they were alive, these animals were firmly attached to hard surfaces by a long stem. Individuals of *Pentacrinites* hung upside down from driftwood. The stems were made of disk-shaped segments, and these are often found fossilized singly or in columns. Sometimes, whole beds of limestone are composed almost entirely of such remains. Most crinoids today do not have stems. Known as feather stars, they crawl and swim using their arms. Stemmed species live only in deep water. They spread out their arms to fan small particles of food toward their mouths. They look a little like flowering plants which is why they are often known as sea lilies. Another group of extinct echinoderms were the blastoids. These looked like stemmed crinoids but did not have arms.

Fossil *Pentacrinites*

Fishes

FISHES are the most primitive vertebrates (animals with backbones). They are a very varied group, with about 20,000 species, and they use gills to breathe and fins to swim. Some fishes live in the sea and some in fresh water; others migrate between these environments. Fishes first appeared about 500 million years ago. Most were small, jawless, and covered with heavy armor. In the Devonian period, often referred to as the Age of Fishes, fishes became numerous, and early representatives of the major living groups were present. Skeletons of fossil fishes can be abundant in certain areas, but it is more common to find isolated teeth, especially of sharks.

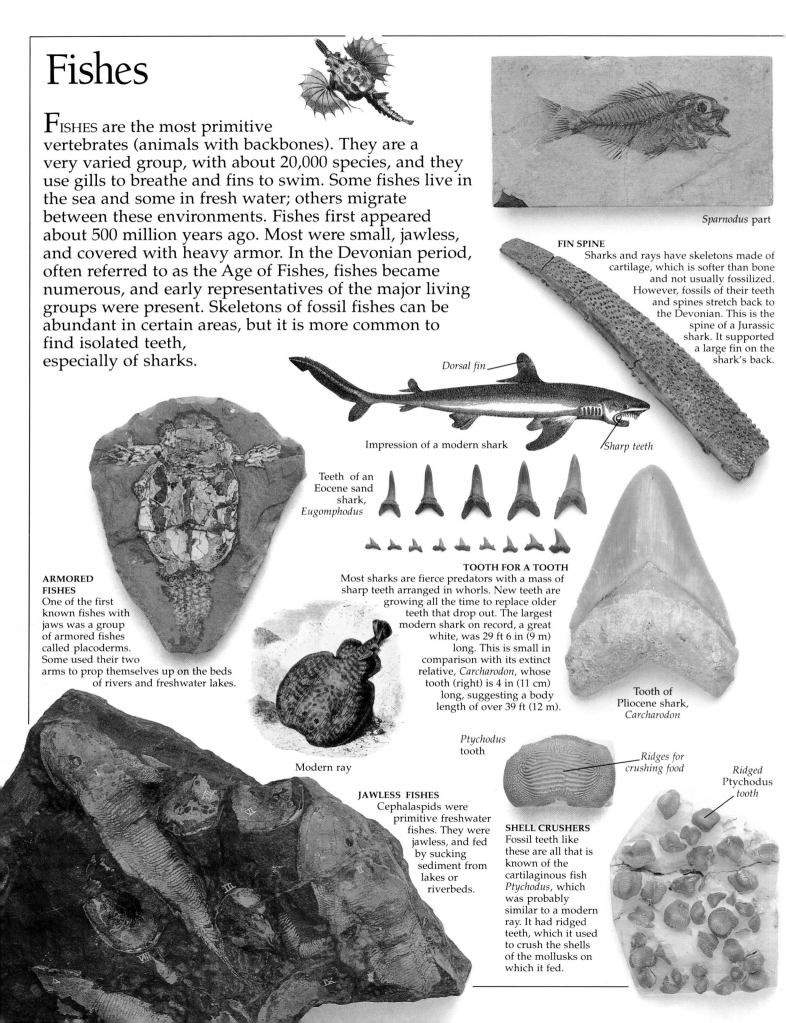

Sparnodus part

FIN SPINE
Sharks and rays have skeletons made of cartilage, which is softer than bone and not usually fossilized. However, fossils of their teeth and spines stretch back to the Devonian. This is the spine of a Jurassic shark. It supported a large fin on the shark's back.

Dorsal fin

Impression of a modern shark

Sharp teeth

Teeth of an Eocene sand shark, *Eugomphodus*

ARMORED FISHES
One of the first known fishes with jaws was a group of armored fishes called placoderms. Some used their two arms to prop themselves up on the beds of rivers and freshwater lakes.

TOOTH FOR A TOOTH
Most sharks are fierce predators with a mass of sharp teeth arranged in whorls. New teeth are growing all the time to replace older teeth that drop out. The largest modern shark on record, a great white, was 29 ft 6 in (9 m) long. This is small in comparison with its extinct relative, *Carcharodon*, whose tooth (right) is 4 in (11 cm) long, suggesting a body length of over 39 ft (12 m).

Tooth of Pliocene shark, *Carcharodon*

Modern ray

Ptychodus tooth

JAWLESS FISHES
Cephalaspids were primitive freshwater fishes. They were jawless, and fed by sucking sediment from lakes or riverbeds.

SHELL CRUSHERS
Fossil teeth like these are all that is known of the cartilaginous fish *Ptychodus*, which was probably similar to a modern ray. It had ridged teeth, which it used to crush the shells of the mollusks on which it fed.

Ridges for crushing food

Ridged *Ptychodus* tooth

Well-preserved skeleton

FISH EATS FISH *right*
Fossils seldom provide direct evidence of an animal's diet. However, this remarkable Cretaceous dogfish contains the head of a teleost that it swallowed. The dogfish had very small teeth and would probably not have been able to bite the head off the body of a live fish. It seems more likely that the dogfish scavenged the head from a dead fish.

Swallowed fish head

Sparnodus counterpart

TWO PARTS
This slab of Eocene limestone has split through a fine fossil specimen of *Sparnodus*. The two pieces are called the part (left) and the counterpart (above). Bones of the skeleton, including the fins, are preserved in remarkable detail. *Sparnodus* belongs to a group of bony fishes still living today, known as porgies or sea breams.

THICK-SCALED FISH
Lepidotes was a Mesozoic bony fish. It was common all over the world, and some examples grew to a length of almost 6 ft 6 in (2 m). The body was covered by thick scales, and the button-shaped teeth, called toadstones in folklore (p. 16), were probably used to crush mollusk shells.

Thick scales covering the body

EAR STONES
Otoliths, or ear stones, are balance organs from the ears of fishes. They are made of chalky material and form unusual fossils. These examples are from Eocene fishes.

Sharp predator's teeth

Modern African lungfish

TEETH FOR HUNTING
Related to the modern bowfin, *Caturus* is from the Jurassic. By the look of its sharp teeth it was a predator.

Thick scales

Armored head

BONY FISHES
About 200 million years ago, this primitive teleost, a type of bony fish, lived in the seas. It had small teeth, which suggests that it fed on tiny plankton, possibly living in schools like today's herring. Teleosts first appeared in the Triassic, and today they are the most common fishes. They include carp, salmon, cod, mackerel, flounder, and many others.

Remains of concretion

EXPOSED WITH ACID
Unlike modern lungfishes, which live in fresh water, the Devonian lungfish *Chirodipterus* lived in shallow seas. It had thick, bony scales and an armored head. This specimen from Australia was preserved in a hard, chalky concretion (p. 9). It has been exposed by treatment in acid, which dissolved the concretion but not the fish within.

Plants-the pioneers

THE INVASION OF THE LAND BY PLANTS about 410 million years ago was a key event in the history of life. It paved the way for colonization by animals and was the starting point for the development of the variety of plants we see today. Plants growing on the land had to be strong enough to support themselves against gravity, resistant to drying, and able to transport water, gathered by the roots, up to the higher portions of the plant where energy-producing photosynthesis occurred. These adaptations were first seen among the primitive land plants such as club mosses, horsetails, and ferns of the late Paleozoic. Examples from all of these groups are living today, though often in greatly reduced numbers. The flowering plants which dominate modern floras did not appear until the Cretaceous.

JET JEWELRY
Jet is a special kind of fossil wood which is dense enough to be carved and polished for jewelry. The formation of jet probably occurred when wood from monkey puzzle trees (opposite) was washed into the sea by rivers.

Impression in sandstone of the bark of *Lepidodendron*

JOHANN SCHEUCHZER
The Swiss naturalist and physician Johann Scheuchzer (1672–1733) studied fossil plants and fishes from the Miocene rocks at Oeningen in Switzerland.

Diamond-shaped leaf scars

Lepidodendron

Cross-section of the fossil cone *Lepidostrobus*

Fossil *Baragwanathia*

Club mosses

Club mosses, which belong to a group of plants called lycopods, reproduce by spores which are held in cones. Lycopods were common during the Paleozoic; *Baragwanathia* from the Devonian of Australia is probably the oldest known example. Some modern club mosses have creeping stems, unlike the Paleozoic lycopods which grew as trees. *Lepidodendron* reached 130 ft (40 m) tall. The fossil bark of *Lepidodendron* has a diamond pattern on it made by scars left when the leaves fell off. The fossil cones of *Lepidodendron* have been named *Lepidostrobus*.

Carboniferous club moss *Archaeosigillaria*

Modern club moss *Lycopodium*

Archaeopteris, an extinct tree which reproduced by spores and grew up to 98 ft (30 m) tall

Modern plant showing fern-like features

Towards the seeds

The oldest ferns are of Devonian age. Club mosses declined after the Paleozoic, but ferns did not. They are common fossils in Mesozoic rocks and about 10,000 species are alive today. They have spore cases on the underside of their leaves. Tree ferns such as *Psaronius* grew alongside club moss trees in the coal forests of the Carboniferous (pp. 40–41). Most modern tree ferns are not closely related to these Paleozoic forms but belong to two families which appeared in the Jurassic. The leaves of the now-extinct seed ferns often resemble true fern leaves but they were, in fact, relatives of more advanced, seed-bearing plants (pp. 38–39).

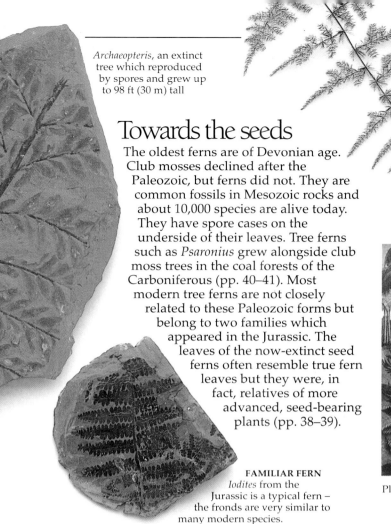

FAMILIAR FERN
Iodites from the Jurassic is a typical fern – the fronds are very similar to many modern species.

Plants in a typical Paleozoic scene

COMPRESSED FERN
Carbonized (turned to coal) leaves of the Jurassic fern *Coniopteris* are here preserved as compressions.

POLISHED FERN
This sectioned and polished piece of fossil wood is from the tree fern *Psaronius*, which grew to a height of 26 ft (8 m).

FOSSIL MONKEY PUZZLE CONES
One cone has been sectioned to show the internal structure.

Leathery leaf

WIDESPREAD SEED FERN
The presence of fossils of this seed fern, *Glossopteris*, in India, Africa, South America, Australia, and Antarctica provides evidence that these areas were once linked together as Gondwanaland (pp. 12–13).

Leaf-bearing part of stem

The only modern horsetail genus, *Equisetum*, which grows to about 5 ft (1.5 m) tall

Modern monkey puzzle branch

MONKEY PUZZLE
The monkey puzzle is a primitive type of conifer (pp. 38–39) first appearing in the Triassic. Today they live in the Andes mountains in South America. The tightly packed leathery leaves may live for 15 years before falling off the branch.

HORSETAILS
Horsetails date from the Devonian. Some grew as trees in the coal forests (pp. 40–41), reaching heights of 60 ft (18 m). This is the stem of a Jurassic *Equisetites*.

Equisetites

Underground part of stem

Continued on next page

Protected seeds

Most modern seed-producing plants have their seeds protected in a fruit (flowering plants, called angiosperms) or a cone (gymnosperms, including conifers). Angiosperms are the most successful of modern plants. There are an estimated 250,000 species, as compared with 50,000 species of all other plants. Grasses, oaks, tulips, palms, potatoes, and cacti are angiosperms. In spite of their great variety, angiosperms appear relatively late in the fossil record. The earliest examples come from the Cretaceous. The earliest conifer fossils occur earlier, in the Carboniferous.

SOFT FRUIT
All fruits contain seeds of some sort. Soft fruits decay quickly. Hard seeds are more likely to be fossilized.

Palm-like leaf

Fossil cycad

BEFORE THE FLOWERS
When angiosperms first appeared, some of the most common plants were cycads – palmlike gymnosperms which produced seeds in separate conelike structures. Modern cycads still look like palms. There are nine kinds living in tropical and subtropical forests.

Sabal *leaf*

Annual rings preserved in stone

Petrified conifer wood

CYCAD COMPANION
Other gymnosperms were also living at this time, and some Cretaceous conifer wood has been petrified (turned to stone). Petrification has preserved remarkable details of the original wood.

FOSSIL PALM
There are two main types of angiosperms - monocotyledons and dicotyledons. Monocotyledons generally have leaves with parallel veins; dicotyledons usually have net-veined leaves. Palms, like this *Sabal* from the Eocene, are monocotyledons, as are grasses. All other angiosperms shown are dicotyledons.

Palm-like tree

Seed

Leaf

"Cone"

Modern cycad

One leaf split horizontally into two parts

SPLIT IN TWO
Angiosperm leaves are relatively common and well preserved in some fine-grained sedimentary rocks. This Miocene example of a myrtle leaf has been fractured into two parts.

Leaf of a modern palm

Fossil *Nipa* fruit

COAST GUARDS
A fruit of a modern *Nipa* tree is compared here with a smaller fossil *Nipa* fruit from the Eocene. *Nipa* is a stemless palm which grows today along tropical coastlines or rivers close to the coast. It plays an important role in preventing coastal erosion.

FLAT CHESTNUT
This is the flattened seed of a water chestnut from the Miocene.

Modern *Nipa* fruit

continued from previous page

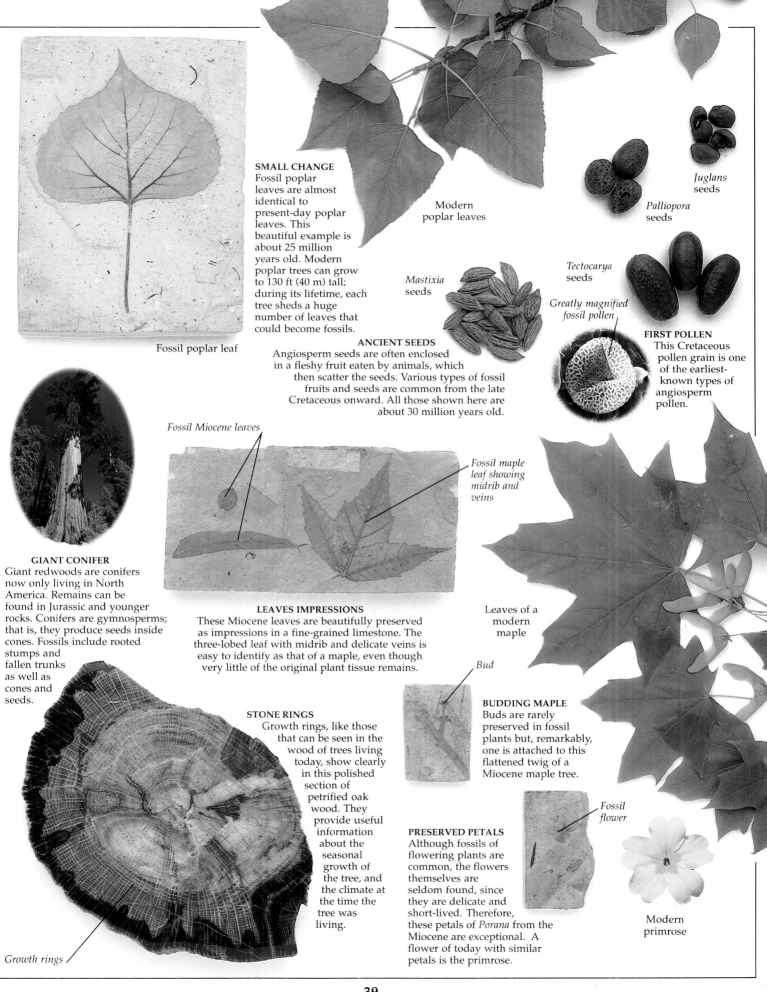

SMALL CHANGE
Fossil poplar leaves are almost identical to present-day poplar leaves. This beautiful example is about 25 million years old. Modern poplar trees can grow to 130 ft (40 m) tall; during its lifetime, each tree sheds a huge number of leaves that could become fossils.

Fossil poplar leaf

Modern poplar leaves

Juglans seeds

Palliopora seeds

Mastixia seeds

Tectocarya seeds

Greatly magnified fossil pollen

ANCIENT SEEDS
Angiosperm seeds are often enclosed in a fleshy fruit eaten by animals, which then scatter the seeds. Various types of fossil fruits and seeds are common from the late Cretaceous onward. All those shown here are about 30 million years old.

FIRST POLLEN
This Cretaceous pollen grain is one of the earliest-known types of angiosperm pollen.

GIANT CONIFER
Giant redwoods are conifers now only living in North America. Remains can be found in Jurassic and younger rocks. Conifers are gymnosperms; that is, they produce seeds inside cones. Fossils include rooted stumps and fallen trunks as well as cones and seeds.

Fossil Miocene leaves

Fossil maple leaf showing midrib and veins

LEAVES IMPRESSIONS
These Miocene leaves are beautifully preserved as impressions in a fine-grained limestone. The three-lobed leaf with midrib and delicate veins is easy to identify as that of a maple, even though very little of the original plant tissue remains.

Leaves of a modern maple

Bud

BUDDING MAPLE
Buds are rarely preserved in fossil plants but, remarkably, one is attached to this flattened twig of a Miocene maple tree.

STONE RINGS
Growth rings, like those that can be seen in the wood of trees living today, show clearly in this polished section of petrified oak wood. They provide useful information about the seasonal growth of the tree, and the climate at the time the tree was living.

Fossil flower

PRESERVED PETALS
Although fossils of flowering plants are common, the flowers themselves are seldom found, since they are delicate and short-lived. Therefore, these petals of *Porana* from the Miocene are exceptional. A flower of today with similar petals is the primrose.

Modern primrose

Growth rings

Fossil fuels

OIL AND COAL are known as fossil fuels because they originate from ancient organisms, mainly plants. When we burn them we release the energy, in the form of heat and light, which was originally captured by the living plants during photosynthesis millions of years ago. Fossil fuels are extracted from the Earth in huge quantities. In addition to being a source of energy, they are also used in the manufacture of many synthetic materials.

A coal forest

Living mosses and grasses

COAL PLANT
This is the impression of the bark of one of the plants which lived in the vast coal forests of the Carboniferous. About two-thirds of the world's coal supplies were formed by the plants of these forests.

PEAT
The plants growing on top of this peat will eventually die and add their rotting remains to the peat beneath. Dried peat is sometimes used as a household fuel.

Crack caused when drying

LIGNITE
Lignite, the first stage of coal formation, is typically dark brown and may still contain some water. Lignite crumbles easily and may crack as it dries in the air.

From plant to coal

Coal is formed after millions of years by the decay and burial of plants that usually grow in freshwater swamps. Special conditions are needed for coal to form. During the early stages of the process, oxygen must not be present so that bacterial decay of the plants can lead to the formation of peat. The peat is then buried and compressed under the weight of more sediment and rotting plants. It undergoes chemical changes resulting first in lignite, then bituminous coal, and finally, if temperatures and pressures become sufficiently high, anthracite coal.

Impression of lycopod bark

BITUMINOUS COAL
Black bituminous coal is sometimes used as a fuel for household heating. The impression of a Carboniferous lycopod tree (p. 36) seen here shows the plant origin of the coal.

MODERN MINING
Most coal is extracted by deep mining. When the coal is near the surface, it is extracted by strip mining.

COAL LABOR
Wagons full of coal were once hauled through the underground tunnels by men, women, and children. Nowadays, there are conveyor belts, or trucks pulled by engines.

Ink

Shoe polish

ALL MADE FROM COAL
Most coal is burned to provide heat or to make steam which, in turn, is used to drive the generators in power stations producing electricity. But many everyday products used in the home and garden are also made from coal. These include coal-tar soap, ink, and shoe polish. Other products sometimes made from coal are antiseptics, drugs, dyes, detergents, perfumes, nail polish, fertilizers, weed-killers, insecticides, nylon, and plastics.

Coal-tar soap

ANTHRACITE
Anthracite is a hard, intensely black and shiny coal. It is the best-quality coal.

OIL PLANT
This is a greatly enlarged fossil of a microscopic Eocene plant which lived in the sea. Similar planktonic plants were the originators of oil. Their fossilized remains provide important clues about rocks, useful to geologists searching for oil.

NO OIL
This core of rock, cut during drilling for geologists to examine, does not contain any oil.

OIL-BEARING
This dark piece of porous core does contain oil. Oil does not form huge underground lakes but is held as tiny droplets in the pores in the rock – as water is held in a sponge.

Light crude oil

REFINED OIL
Oils are treated in a refinery. Refining is a very complex process involving several different stages.

From plankton to oil

Oil and natural gas are together known as petroleum, from the Latin words *petra* (rock) and *oleum* (oil). They were formed mainly by the decomposition of tiny planktonic plants which lived near the surface of the sea. When they died, their remains sank to the sea bed and were buried in mud. Over millions of years, this mud turned to rock, and the organic remains formed specks of carbon-rich kerogen, an early stage of oil, and then oil. Oil is often found some distance away from where it originated. It migrates, or moves, generally upward through porous rocks which have tiny spaces into which it can seep. If it meets an impervious layer of rock – that is, rock which has no pores – the oil cannot migrate. It may therefore become trapped in what is then called a "reservoir rock."

Modern oil rig

Heavy crude oil

CRUDE OILS
It can be extremely difficult to get oil out of rock. Often, the presence of natural gas helps force the oil up to the surface, but sometimes pressure is too low and the oil has to be pumped up. Crude oils – oils in their natural state – vary widely. The heaviest oils, formed at relatively low temperatures, are black, thick, and waxy. The lightest oils, formed at high temperatures, are pale and thin. All crude oils must be refined before they can be used.

Crayons

ALL MADE FROM OIL
Once in the refinery, oil is separated into different liquids, gases, and solids. These are used to make a wide range of products in addition to gasoline, diesel fuel, and lubricating oil. Many detergents, paints, plastics, and clothes are derived from petroleum chemicals. These crayons, sunglasses, and polyester scarf are all byproducts of oil.

Three cones of the bit

DRILLING FOR OIL
The most common drill bit is a tri-cone bit like this one. Bits cut through rock by being rotated at the bottom of a hollow drill pipe down which a muddy fluid is pumped. This fluid lubricates and cools the bit and carries away the fragments of rock.

An early way of drilling for oil

Polyester scarf

Sunglasses

Fossil foraminifers

MICROSCOPIC FOSSILS
Fossils of foraminifers – microscopic animals with chalky shells – are often used by geologists to date rocks.

Out of the water

CURIOUS CREATURE
This curious amphibian, *Diplocaulus*, from the Permian of Texas, lived in ponds and streams.

COLONIZATION OF THE LAND by vertebrates 350 million years ago was made possible through the evolution of lungs for breathing air, and limbs for walking. Air-breathing was inherited by the first land vertebrates, amphibians, from their fish ancestors. Fishes with lungs for breathing – lungfishes (p. 35) – still exist today. The Australian lungfish can gulp fresh air from the surface of drying ponds while other fishes die in the foul water. Limbs for walking developed from muscular fins similar to those seen in the living coelacanth (p. 61). Most amphibians have a larval stage (tadpole) which has to live in water, and for this reason amphibians must return to water to lay their eggs.

Fleshy outline of the body

Long hind legs

FOSSIL FROG
This fossil frog is a female of a species of *Discoglossus*. It comes from the Miocene of West Germany. The specimen is unusual in showing the fleshy outline of the body and long hind legs. Frogs first appeared in the Triassic but are seldom found fossilized because their delicate bones decay very easily.

Eyes

FOSSIL TADPOLE
Even rarer than fossils of adult frogs are fossils of their tadpoles. The two eyes can be clearly seen in this Cenozoic specimen of *Pelobates*.

ETERNAL YOUTH
The axolotl is an unusual salamander from Central America. It remains in a "larval" stage throughout its life, using its feathery external gills to breathe underwater and not coming onto land. The name axolotl comes from an appropriate Aztec word meaning "water doll."

GOING THROUGH STAGES
Like most amphibians, frogs usually have to lay their eggs in water. The eggs hatch into tadpoles which live in the water. As they develop, tadpoles go through different stages before they leave the water as miniature frogs. Lungs replace gills as a means of breathing, front and back legs grow, and the tail gradually disappears.

SURVIVING AMPHIBIAN
The early inhabitants of the land differed in many ways from the amphibians which have survived to the present day such as frogs, toads, newts, and salamanders. This is a modern natterjack toad.

Heavy hip bones

Strong foot

EARLY ANCESTOR
One of the earliest known amphibians, *Ichthyostega*, is found in Devonian rocks in Greenland. It is regarded by some paleontologists as an ancestor of all later amphibians. It was apparently able to walk on land and had lungs for breathing air, but still had a tail fin like a fish.

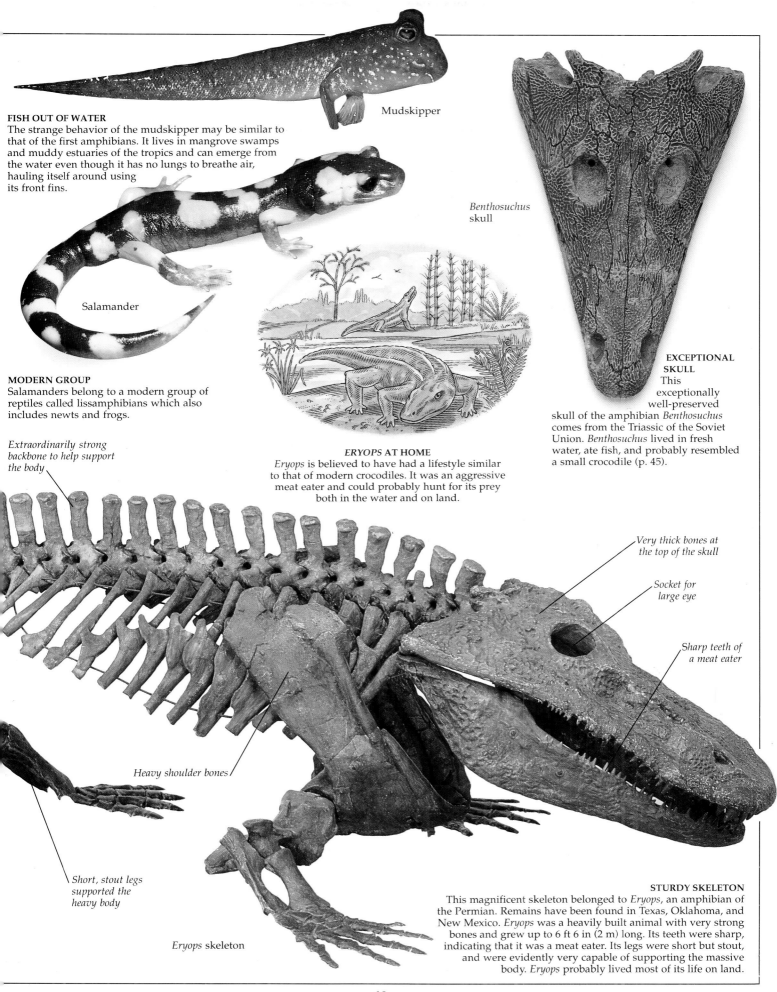

FISH OUT OF WATER
The strange behavior of the mudskipper may be similar to that of the first amphibians. It lives in mangrove swamps and muddy estuaries of the tropics and can emerge from the water even though it has no lungs to breathe air, hauling itself around using its front fins.

Mudskipper

Salamander

Benthosuchus skull

MODERN GROUP
Salamanders belong to a modern group of reptiles called lissamphibians which also includes newts and frogs.

Extraordinarily strong backbone to help support the body

EXCEPTIONAL SKULL
This exceptionally well-preserved skull of the amphibian *Benthosuchus* comes from the Triassic of the Soviet Union. *Benthosuchus* lived in fresh water, ate fish, and probably resembled a small crocodile (p. 45).

***ERYOPS* AT HOME**
Eryops is believed to have had a lifestyle similar to that of modern crocodiles. It was an aggressive meat eater and could probably hunt for its prey both in the water and on land.

Very thick bones at the top of the skull

Socket for large eye

Sharp teeth of a meat eater

Heavy shoulder bones

Short, stout legs supported the heavy body

Eryops skeleton

STURDY SKELETON
This magnificent skeleton belonged to *Eryops*, an amphibian of the Permian. Remains have been found in Texas, Oklahoma, and New Mexico. *Eryops* was a heavily built animal with very strong bones and grew up to 6 ft 6 in (2 m) long. Its teeth were sharp, indicating that it was a meat eater. Its legs were short but stout, and were evidently very capable of supporting the massive body. *Eryops* probably lived most of its life on land.

Onto the land

There are over 2,000 species of snakes living today

THREE MAIN KINDS OF REPTILES live today: lizards and snakes, tortoises and turtles, and crocodiles. A fourth is represented only by the tuatara (p. 60). The number of surviving reptiles is much less than the number of extinct forms, especially those which lived in Mesozoic times such as dinosaurs (pp. 48–51), pterosaurs (p. 52), and ichthyosaurs and plesiosaurs (pp. 46–47). The first reptile fossils are found in rocks from the early Carboniferous, about 300 million years old. It is thought that these early reptiles possessed two important features, still seen in modern species, that enabled them to live away from water unlike amphibians: a special kind of egg, known as an amniote egg (below), and a scaly skin which protected their bodies against drying out.

READY FOR LAND
Turtle eggs contain liquid and are protected by leathery shells. Before birth an embryo can develop through early stages into an animal able to breathe and live on land.

BODY GUARD
Trionyx is a turtle from the Eocene. Only the protective carapace, or shell, is preserved here – the bones are missing. The first turtles appeared in the Triassic and probably lacked the ability of modern species to withdraw their head, limbs, and tail completely. Another difference is that they had teeth, which are replaced in modern species by a sharp, horny beak for slicing vegetation or meat.

BURIED EGGS
Sea-going turtles return to land to lay their eggs, which they bury in the warm sands of tropical beaches, and then return to the sea. The largest living turtle is the leatherback, which may reach 8 ft (2.5 m) in length. The Cretaceous turtle *Archelon* grew to more than 13 ft (4 m) long!

Modern ladder snake

LEGLESS VERTEBRATE
The earliest fossil snakes come from the late Cretaceous. Snakes have a poor fossil record but vertebrae are occasionally found. These vertebrae of *Paleophis*, from the Paleocene of Mali, West Africa, were found separately but have been assembled to give an impression of one snake's backbone. Snakes probably evolved from a lizard-like ancestor, with their limbs getting smaller and smaller and eventually disappearing altogether. This is thought to have been the result of the animal adopting a burrowing lifestyle, which was later abandoned by true snakes. Two important features seen in modern snakes are the poisonous fangs, used to inject venom into prey, and the loosely connected skull bones, which enable the snake to open its mouth very wide to swallow large prey.

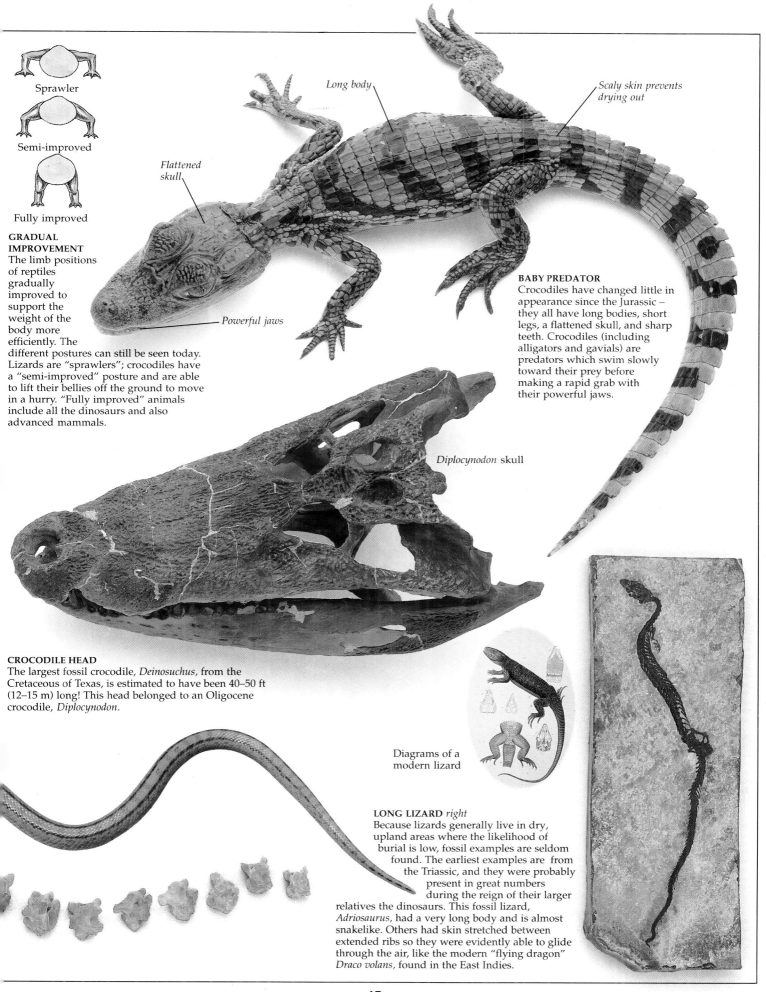

Sprawler

Semi-improved

Fully improved

**GRADUAL
IMPROVEMENT**
The limb positions
of reptiles
gradually
improved to
support the
weight of the
body more
efficiently. The
different postures can still be seen today.
Lizards are "sprawlers"; crocodiles have
a "semi-improved" posture and are able
to lift their bellies off the ground to move
in a hurry. "Fully improved" animals
include all the dinosaurs and also
advanced mammals.

*Flattened
skull*

Long body

*Scaly skin prevents
drying out*

Powerful jaws

BABY PREDATOR
Crocodiles have changed little in
appearance since the Jurassic –
they all have long bodies, short
legs, a flattened skull, and sharp
teeth. Crocodiles (including
alligators and gavials) are
predators which swim slowly
toward their prey before
making a rapid grab with
their powerful jaws.

Diplocynodon skull

CROCODILE HEAD
The largest fossil crocodile, *Deinosuchus*, from the
Cretaceous of Texas, is estimated to have been 40–50 ft
(12–15 m) long! This head belonged to an Oligocene
crocodile, *Diplocynodon*.

Diagrams of a
modern lizard

LONG LIZARD *right*
Because lizards generally live in dry,
upland areas where the likelihood of
burial is low, fossil examples are seldom
found. The earliest examples are from
the Triassic, and they were probably
present in great numbers
during the reign of their larger
relatives the dinosaurs. This fossil lizard,
Adriosaurus, had a very long body and is almost
snakelike. Others had skin stretched between
extended ribs so they were evidently able to glide
through the air, like the modern "flying dragon"
Draco volans, found in the East Indies.

Sea dragons

DURING MESOZOIC TIMES, when dinosaurs roamed the land, the seas were inhabited by several kinds of giant reptiles popularly known as sea dragons. The most numerous of these were the ichthyosaurs and plesiosaurs; a third group, the mosasaurs, became common toward the end of the Mesozoic. None of these marine reptiles was really a dragon, of course, but their remains may have contributed to the legends of the long-necked, fire-breathing monsters. Their ways of life were similar to modern marine mammals such as small whales, dolphins, and seals. Some were fish eaters; others ate belemnites (p. 29) and other mollusks (pp. 26–29). They all breathed air and were therefore forced to surface regularly. Ichthyosaurs, plesiosaurs, and mosasaurs all became extinct, as did the dinosaurs, about 65 million years ago at the end of the Cretaceous.

MARY ANNING
Mary Anning (1799–1847) is famous for the fossils she collected close to her home in Lyme Regis on the south coast of England. The cliffs here contain abundant fossils of animals which lived in the sea in Jurassic times. Between 1810 and 1812 Mary and her brother excavated a complete ichthyosaur (at the time thought to be a crocodile) which they sold for £23, a large sum of money in those days.

A GOOD LIKENESS
The similarity in shape between modern dolphins and ichthyosaurs suggests they had a similar lifestyle.

Dorsal fin for steering

Backbone

Kink in backbone

Powerful tail for swimming

Pointed tooth

A mosasaur

Excavation of a mosasaur jaw from a chalk mine at Maastricht in the Netherlands, in the 18th century.

JAW OF A GIANT LIZARD
Three pointed teeth are visible in this fragment of a mosasaur jaw from the Cretaceous. Mosasaurs were closely related to the land-dwelling monitor lizards of today. Mosasaurs grew up to 30 ft (9 m) long, and were probably slow-moving predators. They existed for a relatively short time in geological history, being known only from the late Cretaceous.

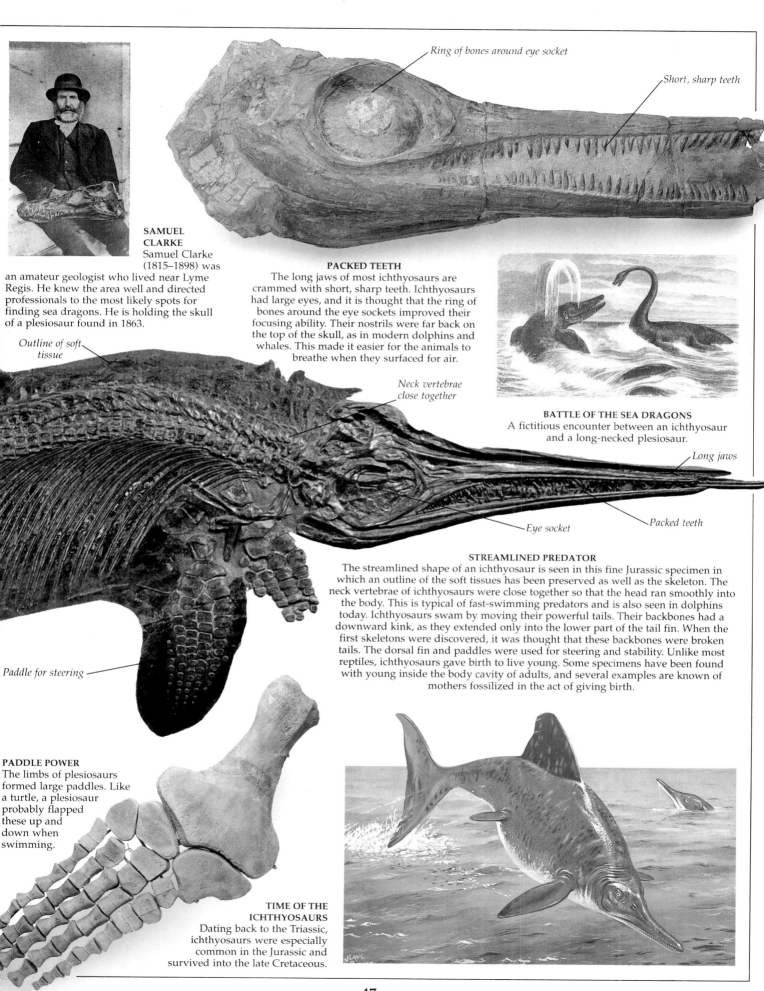

Ring of bones around eye socket

Short, sharp teeth

SAMUEL CLARKE

Samuel Clarke (1815–1898) was an amateur geologist who lived near Lyme Regis. He knew the area well and directed professionals to the most likely spots for finding sea dragons. He is holding the skull of a plesiosaur found in 1863.

PACKED TEETH

The long jaws of most ichthyosaurs are crammed with short, sharp teeth. Ichthyosaurs had large eyes, and it is thought that the ring of bones around the eye sockets improved their focusing ability. Their nostrils were far back on the top of the skull, as in modern dolphins and whales. This made it easier for the animals to breathe when they surfaced for air.

BATTLE OF THE SEA DRAGONS

A fictitious encounter between an ichthyosaur and a long-necked plesiosaur.

Outline of soft tissue

Neck vertebrae close together

Long jaws

Eye socket

Packed teeth

Paddle for steering

STREAMLINED PREDATOR

The streamlined shape of an ichthyosaur is seen in this fine Jurassic specimen in which an outline of the soft tissues has been preserved as well as the skeleton. The neck vertebrae of ichthyosaurs were close together so that the head ran smoothly into the body. This is typical of fast-swimming predators and is also seen in dolphins today. Ichthyosaurs swam by moving their powerful tails. Their backbones had a downward kink, as they extended only into the lower part of the tail fin. When the first skeletons were discovered, it was thought that these backbones were broken tails. The dorsal fin and paddles were used for steering and stability. Unlike most reptiles, ichthyosaurs gave birth to live young. Some specimens have been found with young inside the body cavity of adults, and several examples are known of mothers fossilized in the act of giving birth.

PADDLE POWER

The limbs of plesiosaurs formed large paddles. Like a turtle, a plesiosaur probably flapped these up and down when swimming.

TIME OF THE ICHTHYOSAURS

Dating back to the Triassic, ichthyosaurs were especially common in the Jurassic and survived into the late Cretaceous.

Fossil giants

THERE WERE MANY different species of dinosaurs, and their reign spanned 150 million years from the Triassic to the end of the Cretaceous. Dinosaurs were reptiles. Not all of them were huge; there were large ones and small ones. Some were plant eaters, others were meat eaters. Some had armored plates, others had spiked or clubbed tails. The variety was enormous. We know about dinosaurs from their skeletons, and detailed restorations of them can be made from their bones (p. 14). We cannot know for certain what color they were but can make a guess based on the color of reptiles living today. The mystery of dinosaur extinction at the end of Cretaceous times has stimulated many different theories. Some scientists attribute the extinction to a change in the climate; others, to a change in the vegetation. Whatever the reason, the dinosaurs did not all die out at once. By the end of the Cretaceous, they were already reduced from hundreds of species to fewer than twenty.

FOOD GRINDER
Apatosaurus, a large Jurassic sauropod, weighed about 30 tons. Like all sauropods, it was a plant eater, probably using its long neck to reach leaves on trees. Its teeth were relatively small, and it is thought that *Apatosaurus* swallowed stones which then acted as a mill, grinding up the food in its stomach. Modern crocodiles use stones in a similar way.

MONSTER-STALKING
Although all the giant Mesozoic reptiles became extinct long before humans appeared, some people still search for living examples of these monsters.

Edmontosaurus

PLANT EATER
One of the last-surviving dinosaurs was *Edmontosaurus*. It was a hadrosaur, or duckbill, which grew to about 43 ft (13 m) long. Hadrosaurs were once thought to live partly in water, feeding on water plants, but land-plant fossils have been found with some skeletons, which suggests that a diet of trees and shrubs was more likely. These were dealt with by powerful teeth – about 1,000 in *Edmontosaurus*. Hadrosaurs laid their eggs in mound-shaped nests. A colony of closely grouped hadrosaur nests was discovered in Montana, indicating that the animals may have lived in herds. The nests had young of different ages in them so the adults apparently protected their young.

Skull of *Edmontosaurus*

Powerful teeth for crushing leaves

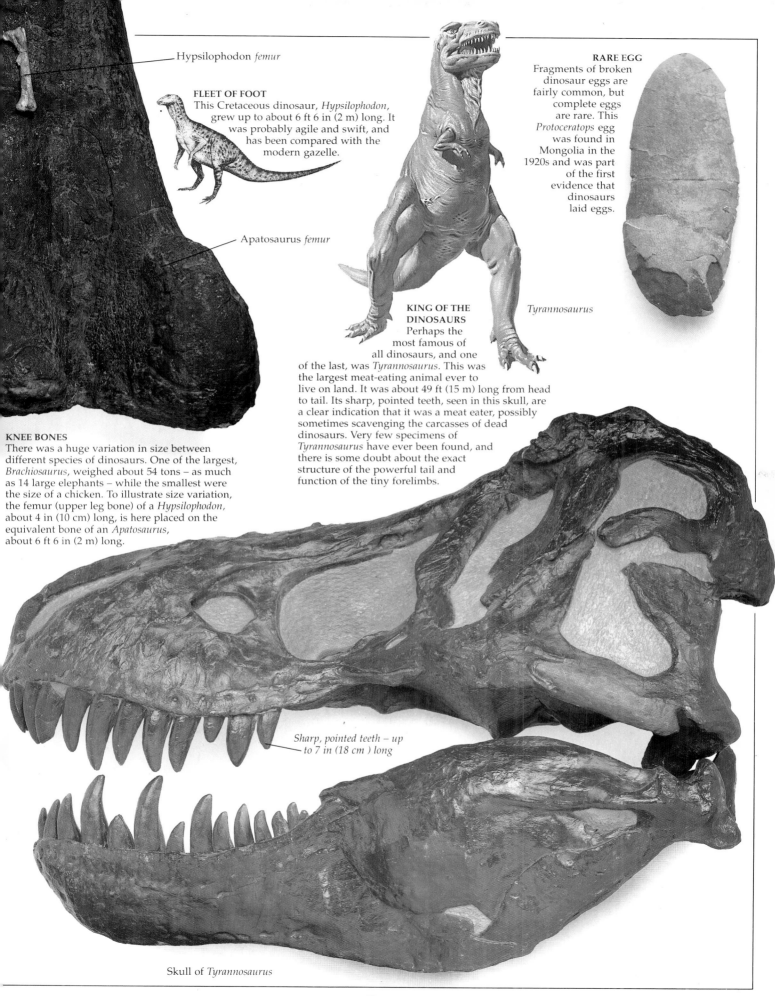

Hypsilophodon *femur*

FLEET OF FOOT
This Cretaceous dinosaur, *Hypsilophodon*, grew up to about 6 ft 6 in (2 m) long. It was probably agile and swift, and has been compared with the modern gazelle.

Apatosaurus *femur*

RARE EGG
Fragments of broken dinosaur eggs are fairly common, but complete eggs are rare. This *Protoceratops* egg was found in Mongolia in the 1920s and was part of the first evidence that dinosaurs laid eggs.

KING OF THE DINOSAURS
Perhaps the most famous of all dinosaurs, and one of the last, was *Tyrannosaurus*. This was the largest meat-eating animal ever to live on land. It was about 49 ft (15 m) long from head to tail. Its sharp, pointed teeth, seen in this skull, are a clear indication that it was a meat eater, possibly sometimes scavenging the carcasses of dead dinosaurs. Very few specimens of *Tyrannosaurus* have ever been found, and there is some doubt about the exact structure of the powerful tail and function of the tiny forelimbs.

Tyrannosaurus

KNEE BONES
There was a huge variation in size between different species of dinosaurs. One of the largest, *Brachiosaurus*, weighed about 54 tons – as much as 14 large elephants – while the smallest were the size of a chicken. To illustrate size variation, the femur (upper leg bone) of a *Hypsilophodon*, about 4 in (10 cm) long, is here placed on the equivalent bone of an *Apatosaurus*, about 6 ft 6 in (2 m) long.

Sharp, pointed teeth – up to 7 in (18 cm) long

Skull of *Tyrannosaurus*

Discovering dinosaurs

Iguanodon *tooth*

MANTELL'S TOOTH!
This is one of the original *Iguanodon* teeth which were named by Mantell in 1825.

THE FIRST DESCRIPTIONS of the fossil bones of dinosaurs were made over 150 years ago. First some teeth and then some bones of *Iguanodon* were found in southern England by the English doctor Gideon Mantell and his wife. Later, bones of the dinosaurs *Megalosaurus* and *Hylaeosaurus* were also discovered. In 1841, Sir Richard Owen, a leading British anatomist, invented the name dinosaur, which means "terrible lizard," for these early discoveries. They were followed by many more all around the world. Huge numbers of dinosaur remains were found in North America during the second half of the 19th century and into the 20th century, and other significant finds were made in Tanzania, China, and Mongolia. Important dinosaur discoveries are still being made of species already known and of new species. Almost every new discovery adds to our knowledge of these magnificent extinct reptiles.

MANTELL'S QUARRY
Mantell was a doctor of medicine and an enthusiastic collector of fossils. The *Iguanodon* teeth and bones he described came from an old quarry in the Cuckfield area of southern England. Here rocks of early Cretaceous age were dug for use as gravel.

BIG REPTILE
In 1824, William Buckland discovered some dinosaur bones in Stonesfield in Oxfordshire, England. He gave the animal the name *Megalosaurus,* which means "big reptile." Buckland was a teacher of geology at the University of Oxford when he described his dinosaur. This jawbone belonged to a *Megalosaurus* and comes from the same area as Buckland's specimens.

BIG BUT NOT BIGGEST
Megalosaurus was a Jurassic meat eater related to the larger and better known *Tyrannosaurus* (p. 49).

EDWARD DRINKER COPE
Between 1870 and 1897 Cope took part in what has been described as the great dinosaur gold rush. It took place in the U.S., primarily in the states of Montana and Wyoming. Two names are especially associated with this gold rush - Cope and Marsh. Each hired independent teams of collectors to excavate dinosaur bones in the race to be first to describe the many new species.

OTHNIEL CHARLES MARSH
In this cartoon, Marsh is depicted as a circus ringmaster leading his team of prehistoric animals. The intense rivalry between Cope and Marsh caused the two men to swap a succession of insults, and even to destroy incomplete fossils in their own quarries in order to prevent future collection by their rival!

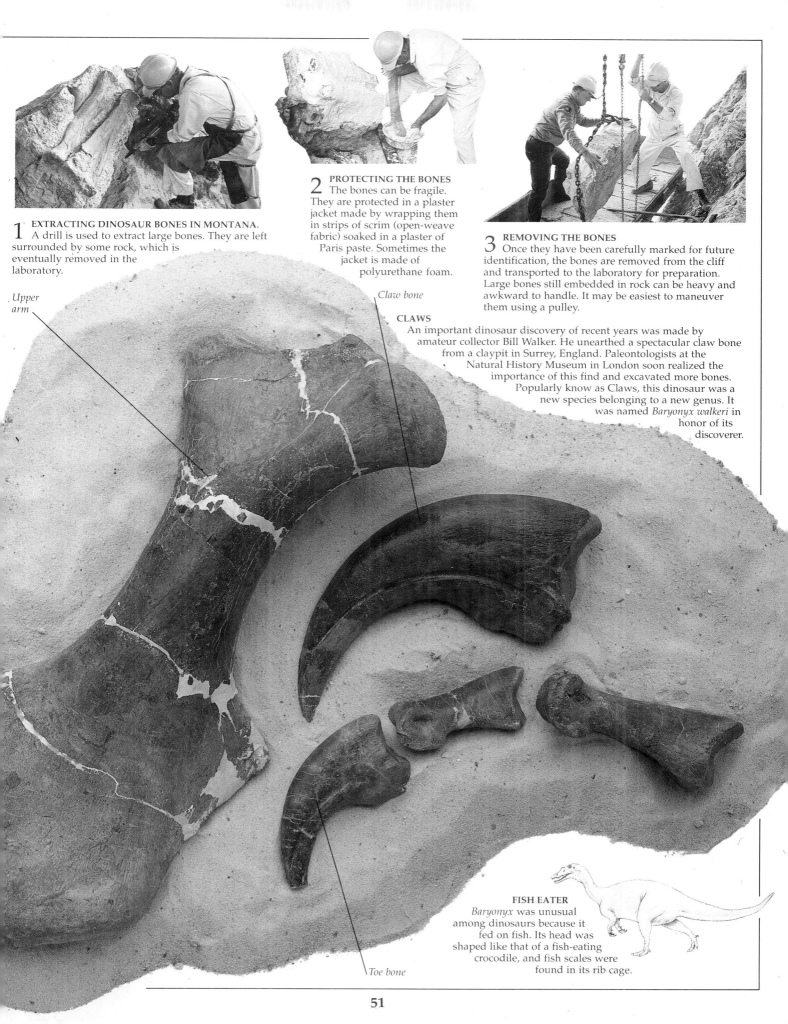

1 EXTRACTING DINOSAUR BONES IN MONTANA.
A drill is used to extract large bones. They are left surrounded by some rock, which is eventually removed in the laboratory.

2 PROTECTING THE BONES
The bones can be fragile. They are protected in a plaster jacket made by wrapping them in strips of scrim (open-weave fabric) soaked in a plaster of Paris paste. Sometimes the jacket is made of polyurethane foam.

3 REMOVING THE BONES
Once they have been carefully marked for future identification, the bones are removed from the cliff and transported to the laboratory for preparation. Large bones still embedded in rock can be heavy and awkward to handle. It may be easiest to maneuver them using a pulley.

CLAWS
An important dinosaur discovery of recent years was made by amateur collector Bill Walker. He unearthed a spectacular claw bone from a claypit in Surrey, England. Paleontologists at the Natural History Museum in London soon realized the importance of this find and excavated more bones. Popularly know as Claws, this dinosaur was a new species belonging to a new genus. It was named *Baryonyx walkeri* in honor of its discoverer.

Upper arm

Claw bone

FISH EATER
Baryonyx was unusual among dinosaurs because it fed on fish. Its head was shaped like that of a fish-eating crocodile, and fish scales were found in its rib cage.

Toe bone

Winged wonders

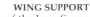

THE FIRST ANIMALS TO FLY were insects; fossil dragonflies have been found in rocks more than 300 million years old. Flying vertebrates appeared almost 100 million years later. True flapping flight has evolved in three groups of vertebrates: pterosaurs (extinct), bats, and birds. They are not closely related, and their ability to fly has evolved independently. Pterosaurs were reptiles, related to dinosaurs (pp. 48–51), with a greatly lengthened fourth finger. This supported the fleshy membrane, a thin sheet of muscle and elastic fibers covered by skin, which was the wing. In birds, the feathered wing is supported by several fingers and the lower part of the forearm. Bats are flying mammals and have wings made of a fleshy membrane similar to that of pterosaurs but supported by four fingers. Because bones of flying vertebrates have to be light, they are fragile and are seldom fossilized.

IMAGINARY BIRD
The finding of pterosaur remains fueled the imagination of authors of science fiction stories.

WING SUPPORT
This is one of the long finger bones which supported the wing of a *Pteranodon*, one of the largest flying animals that ever lived. The wingspan of this Cretaceous pterosaur was about 23 ft (7 m).

WELL-BALANCED
Pteranodon was a pterosaur with a bony crest on its head which counterbalanced its long toothless beak. It appears to have been a fish eater which soared over the oceans like the modern albatross.

FURRY REPTILE
The small Jurassic pterosaur *Pterodactylus* had membranous wings, claws, a toothed beak, and a body covered by fine fur. Evidence for fur comes from some pterosaurs with hair-like impressions around the body which were discovered in Kazakhstan (the Soviet Union). This may indicate that pterosaurs were warm-blooded and the fur acted as insulation. The tail of *Pterodactylus* was short, and its wingspan was only about 20 in (50 cm), but some pterosaurs, including *Rhamphorhynchus* with a wingspan of 5 ft (1.5 m), had long tails. Pterosaurs first appeared during the Triassic and became extinct at the end of the Cretaceous.

Toothed beak

Greatly lengthened fourth finger

Membranous wing

Short tail

Body covered by fine fur

Claws

MISTAKEN IDENTITY
This small dinosaur belongs to a group which many scientists believe were ancestors of birds. In 1973, some museum paleontologists in Germany realized that one of their specimens, long identified as *Compsognathus*, was really an *Archaeopteryx*!

FLYING MAMMAL
It is easy to see the similarity between this bat and the pterosaurs. Bats date from the Eocene. Because bats often roost in caves, their fossil bones can be found in large numbers in cave deposits.

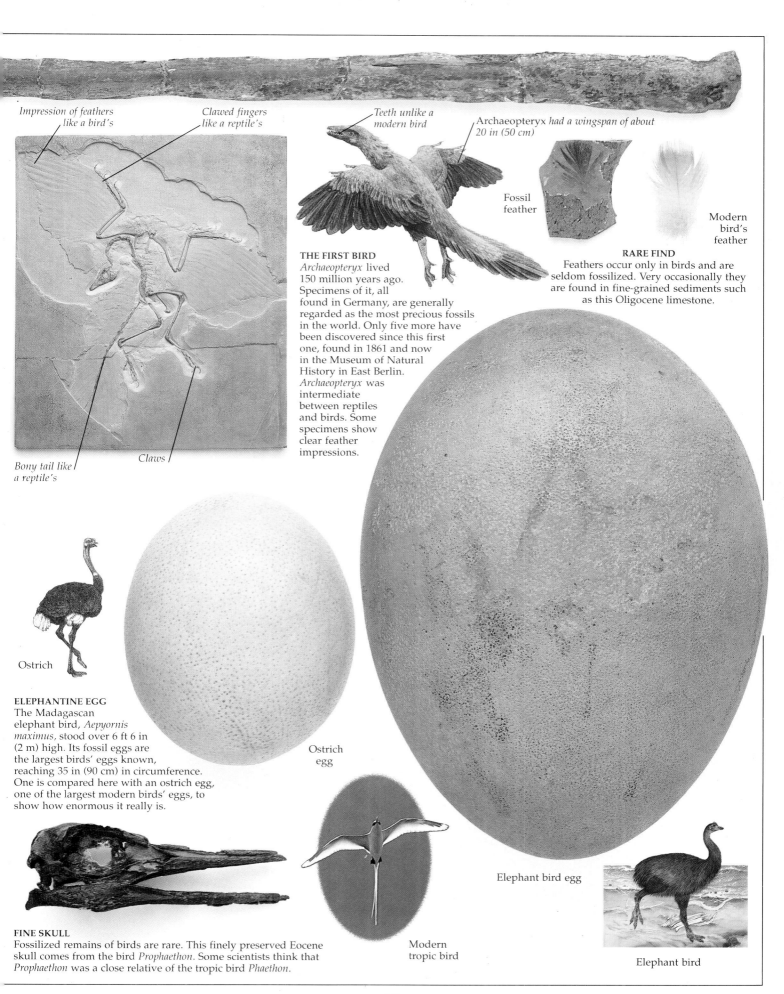

Impression of feathers like a bird's

Clawed fingers like a reptile's

Teeth unlike a modern bird

Archaeopteryx had a wingspan of about 20 in (50 cm)

Fossil feather

Modern bird's feather

THE FIRST BIRD
Archaeopteryx lived 150 million years ago. Specimens of it, all found in Germany, are generally regarded as the most precious fossils in the world. Only five more have been discovered since this first one, found in 1861 and now in the Museum of Natural History in East Berlin. *Archaeopteryx* was intermediate between reptiles and birds. Some specimens show clear feather impressions.

RARE FIND
Feathers occur only in birds and are seldom fossilized. Very occasionally they are found in fine-grained sediments such as this Oligocene limestone.

Bony tail like a reptile's

Claws

Ostrich

ELEPHANTINE EGG
The Madagascan elephant bird, *Aepyornis maximus*, stood over 6 ft 6 in (2 m) high. Its fossil eggs are the largest birds' eggs known, reaching 35 in (90 cm) in circumference. One is compared here with an ostrich egg, one of the largest modern birds' eggs, to show how enormous it really is.

Ostrich egg

Elephant bird egg

FINE SKULL
Fossilized remains of birds are rare. This finely preserved Eocene skull comes from the bird *Prophaethon*. Some scientists think that *Prophaethon* was a close relative of the tropic bird *Phaethon*.

Modern tropic bird

Elephant bird

Mammal variety

ANIMALS AS VARIED AS MICE, ELEPHANTS, kangaroos, bats, cats, whales, horses, and humans are all mammals. They are warm-blooded and produce milk to suckle their infants. Most give birth to live young, have hairy skin and complex teeth, and are highly active. A mammal whose babies develop inside the mother's womb, such as a cat, is known as a placental mammal. The babies of marsupial mammals (pp. 56–57), such as the kangaroo, develop inside the mother's pouch after birth. The first mammals appeared at about the same time as the earliest dinosaurs, 200 million years ago. Nearly all Mesozoic mammals were small shrew-like animals, but in the Cenozoic they diversified into the many different types we are familiar with today. Complete fossil mammals are rare; many species are known only from their teeth. Nevertheless, from these it is possible to build up a picture of the variety of species, what they ate, and the way they lived.

Chisel-like incisor teeth

Skull of *Ischyromys*

Berries

RODENTS
Rodents include rats, mice, and squirrels, and are among the most diverse of mammals. Their large chisel-like incisor teeth grow continuously during life and are used to gnaw a variety of foods. Rodents date from Paleocene times. This example is *Ischyromys* from the famous Oligocene mammal beds of the Badlands in South Dakota.

Modern squirrel

Ants

Skull of *Orycteropus*

INSECT EATERS
Insect-eating mammals are generally small and include shrews and moles. *Orycteropus* was a Miocene aardvark, a peculiar kind of anteater. Mammals living on a diet of ants have several features in common, including a long hard palate in the roof of the mouth which helps prevent ants from entering the windpipe.

Modern aardvark

High-crowned cheek teeth

Modern camel

ICE AGE MAMMAL
Mammoths were elephant-like mammals adapted to life in cold climates during the Pleistocene Ice Ages. Some skeletons have been found preserved in the frozen ground of Siberia (p. 20).

Skull of *Cainotherium*

PLANT EATERS
Many herbivorous mammals, which feed on vegetation, have cheek teeth with high crowns capable of withstanding wear caused by constant chewing. They can be divided into browsers, which eat mostly leaves, and grazers, which eat mostly grass. This skull belonged to *Cainotherium*, a rabbit-like browser whose closest, but very distant, living relative is probably the camel.

Ridges of hard enamel

GRINDING TOOTH
Mammoths were enormous and needed to eat large quantities of vegetation. Their huge high-crowned cheek teeth had ridges of hard enamel on the grinding surface. This enabled them to grind up vegetation with great efficiency.

Leaves

Skull of *Proconsul*

Blunt teeth typical of a fruit eater

Modern monkey

FRUIT EATERS
Monkeys, apes, and humans belong to a group of mammals called the primates. Many primates are omnivores (*omni* means "all") and have a mixed diet, but some eat mostly fruit. Shown here is the skull of the Miocene ape *Proconsul*. The blunt teeth are typical of fruit eaters. As fruit is poor in protein, *Proconsul* may have supplemented its diet with leaves from the trees in which it lived.

Fruit

Nuts

EOCENE LANDSCAPE
Mammals first became common in the Eocene. Many of the mammals which roamed the land belonged to groups with no living descendants.

Skull of *Hoplophoneus*

Large canine tooth

Meat

Sabertooth cat

MEAT EATERS
Carnivorous or meat-eating mammals have large canine teeth. These were developed to their greatest extent in the upper jaws of the so-called sabertooths. They may have used their long teeth to stab the necks of their prey. This skull belongs to *Hoplophoneus* from the Oligocene. Unfortunately, none of the several different sorts of sabertooth known from the fossil record have survived to the present day.

Canine tooth

Skull of *Potamotherium*

FISH EATERS
Potamotherium lived in freshwater lakes during the early Miocene and fed on fish. It was similar to a modern otter but was better adapted to life in water than otters. It may have been a forerunner of seals, which first became common in the sea during the late Miocene.

Fish

Modern otters

A world apart

A boxing kangaroo

AUSTRALIA IS AN ISLAND CONTINENT. The geological record shows that it has been isolated for 50 million years, ever since plate movements caused the continent to drift away from Antarctica (pp. 12–13). This is the reason many of the native mammals in Australia are marsupials. Marsupials differ from other mammals in having pouches in which the young are reared for a period after birth. The fleshy pouches do not fossilize, but there are features of the bones and teeth which distinguish fossils of marsupials from those of placentals (pp. 54–55). Marsupials evolved on their own, away from the placental mammals which came to dominate over them in other parts of the world. Fossils of many extinct marsupials have been found, including *Diprotodon*, the centerpiece of this spread. There are still many species of marsupials in Australia, including the kangaroo and the koala. Other native mammals unique to the country include the extraordinary egg-laying monotremes – the platypus and the echidna.

60 million years ago

Australia

Antarctica

45 million years ago

Australia

Antarctica

DRIFTING CONTINENTS
These two maps show the position of Australia about 60 million years ago (top) and 45 million years ago (bottom) after the split from Antarctica. The isolation of Australia prevented its colonization by placental mammals, apart from some bats and rodents. These might otherwise have replaced the native marsupials. This is probably what happened to the marsupials of South America, such as the extinct sabertooth *Thylacosmilus*, when placental mammals invaded South America after North and South America were joined.

Hip bone connecting the leg to the spine

Marsupial bones which helped support the pouch

Tail vertebrae

TWO FRONT TEETH
This magnificent skeleton of the extinct marsupial *Diprotodon* is about 10 ft (3 m) long. Its name, meaning "two front teeth," refers to the large rodent-like incisors which were used for cropping vegetation. Note the pair of marsupial bones in the pelvic area which can be used to distinguish marsupial from placental mammals. *Diprotodon* comes from Pleistocene rocks and many skeletons have been excavated from Lake Callabonna, a dried-up lake in South Australia. It is possible that *Diprotodon* survived until more recent times and was hunted by early Australians – some animals in ancient Aboriginal paintings could be *Diprotodon*.

GIANT WOMBAT?
Diprotodon (above) was a herbivore. It probably looked like a long-legged wombat (opposite).

Spine, the main
support for the body

Blunt teeth for
grinding vegetation

Rodent-like incisors
for cropping vegetation

Rib cage which
protected the
heart and lungs

Placental mammals

Wolf

Ocelot

Ground hog

Australian marsupials

Tasmanian wolf

Native cat

Wombat

THE OUTBACK
The climate of Australia in the Pliocene became
drier and grasslands spread at the expense of
forests. The Australian outback is now dry and
inhospitable for humans. However, many native
species of mammals thrive there, and parts of
Australia may have been equally inhospitable
when *Diprotodon* lived.

Procoptodon

Young
kangaroo in
the pouch

Modern
kangaroo

ALIKE BUT DIFFERENT
A remarkable feature of mammal evolution is that
for many placental mammals there is an
equivalent marsupial mammal in Australia.
This is called parallel evolution, and it
happened because the animals adapted
to similar ways of life. The placental wolf
which lives on all other continents is
matched in Australia by a marsupial called the
Tasmanian wolf. Sadly the Tasmanian wolf became
extinct about 50 years ago.

A FAKE?
When the remains of a platypus were first
brought to London in the 18th
century, they were dismissed
as a fake! The platypus lives
in fresh water and has fur, webbed feet,
and a beak. It lays eggs but suckles its young.
It may show an early stage in mammal development.

GIANT KANGAROO
Large grazing kangaroos did not become
common until the Pliocene, but the ancestors of
modern kangaroos can be traced back to the
Miocene. *Procoptodon,* a kangaroo of the
Pleistocene, was 10 ft (3 m) tall! A species of
modern kangaroo reaches about 6 ft 6 in (2 m)
when extended to its full height.

Human fossils

Fᴏssɪʟs ᴏғ ᴘᴇᴏᴘʟᴇ (hominids) are rare and fragmentary, but they have been found in increasing numbers during the past few years. They tell us a great deal about the origin and development of modern people. The story begins with the ape-like *Australopithecus* and ends with *Homo sapiens sapiens*. The nearest living relatives of humans are the African Great Apes (chimpanzees and gorillas), but there are many differences between us and them. These include a larger brain in humans and the ability to walk on two legs rather than four legs. Study of fossil hominids shows how these differences developed through geological time. Typical human features first appeared in *Australopithecus*, distinguishing them from their even more ape-like ancestors.

"Bullet hole"

SHOT BY AN ALIEN?
This skull from Broken Hill, Zambia (southern Africa), belongs to an early form of our own species, *Homo sapiens*. It is famous for its bad teeth and the hole in one side. An imaginative writer interpreted this as a hole made by a bullet shot by a visitor from another planet 120,000 years ago! In fact it is a partly healed abscess.

Adult's footprint

Child's footprint

FIRST STEPS
At some stage in human evolution, bipedalism (standing upright and walking on two legs) developed. These footprints from Tanzania (East Africa) were made by two-footed hominids 3.6 million years ago. They were probably two adults and a child *Australopithecus* who walked across a surface of damp volcanic ash. The ash hardened and was buried beneath more ash and sediment. The fossil footprints were discovered by a team led by Mary Leakey in 1977. They prove that a species of primate walked on two feet at least 3.6 million years ago. This ties in with evidence from fossil bones that *Australopithecus* walked on two legs.

Chimpanzee skull

COMPARING FEATURES
These skulls of a modern human and an ape – a chimpanzee – look very similar, but careful comparison shows some of the differences. Humans have much larger brains than chimps. The average volume of a human's brain is 1,400 cc; a chimp's brain is about 400 cc. This is reflected in the domed human cranium, necessary to house the large brain, compared with the low chimp cranium. Another obvious difference is the flatter muzzle of the human. The teeth are also different. For example, a chimp cannot move its jaws from side to side so much when it is chewing, because its canine teeth overlap.

Human skull

Carved reindeer

ARTISTIC BEGINNINGS
This sculpted antler is over 12,000 years old and shows a male reindeer following a female reindeer. It was probably carved using simple flint tools and reveals a high quality of craftsmanship. Such art forms show the development of the cultural activities (art, literature, music, etc) which are unique to humans.

Using a stone to
chip off flakes

THE OLDEST TOOLS
The human being is often described as
the toolmaker. This pebble tool is one of
the oldest recognizable stone tools,
thought to have been made by
Homo habilis ("handy man")
almost 2 million years ago. The
flint handaxe is about
200,000 years old.
Both tools were made
by chipping off flakes
to sharpen them.

Pebble
tool

Flint handaxe

SOUTHERN APE
Several sorts of *Australopithecus*
("southern ape") lived in Africa
between about 5 and 1.5 million
years ago. Certain species were heavily
built and had bony crests on their skulls. Others
were lightly built, like this example from South
Africa. It is possible that these forms are direct
ancestors of modern humans.

LOUIS LEAKEY
The oldest hominids have been found in South
and East Africa. Among the paleontologists
responsible for their discovery have been the
Leakey family – the late Louis Leakey, his wife,
Mary, and their son, Richard.
Louis, pictured here, is
known especially for his
finds of *Australopithecus* at
Olduvai Gorge in Tanzania.

LUCY
This is the
skeleton of an
adult female
Australopithecus. It
was discovered in 1974 and
named after the Beatles' song
"Lucy in the Sky with Diamonds."

Carved animal
head

Harpoon

UPRIGHT MAN
Homo erectus ("upright man") has been found
not only in Africa but also in Southeast Asia.
They lived between about 1.6 million and 500,000
years ago. The size of the cranium indicates a brain size of about
1,000 cc, larger than *Australopithecus* but smaller than modern
humans. *Homo erectus* used fire. An example from China – Peking
Man – was found in a cave deposit with a fossilized hearth that was
used for either cooking
or providing heat
and light.

ROCK PAINTING
These paintings of animals
were done by early people
living in what is now
Algeria (Northwest Africa).

Sickle

Arrowheads

Sharp
flint
pieces

HUNTING TOOLS
These 4,000-year-old arrowheads are made
of flint, a rock favored by early people
because of the ease with which flakes could
be struck off to shape different tools. The
10,000-year-old sickle is made of goat horn
with sharp pieces of flint embedded to form
a cutting edge. The barbed harpoon was
carved from an antler.

ICE AGE RELATIVE
Neanderthals lived in Europe and western
Asia before and during the last Ice Age, between
100,000 and 35,000 years ago. They were given the name because the first
specimen to be described was found in a cave in the Neander valley in Germany.
The brutish caveman image often given to Neanderthals is incorrect. They are
generally thought of as a subspecies of *Homo sapiens* ("thinking man") and
probably looked quite similar to people today. They were stockily built and well
adapted to life in cold climates, with a brain larger on average than our own.

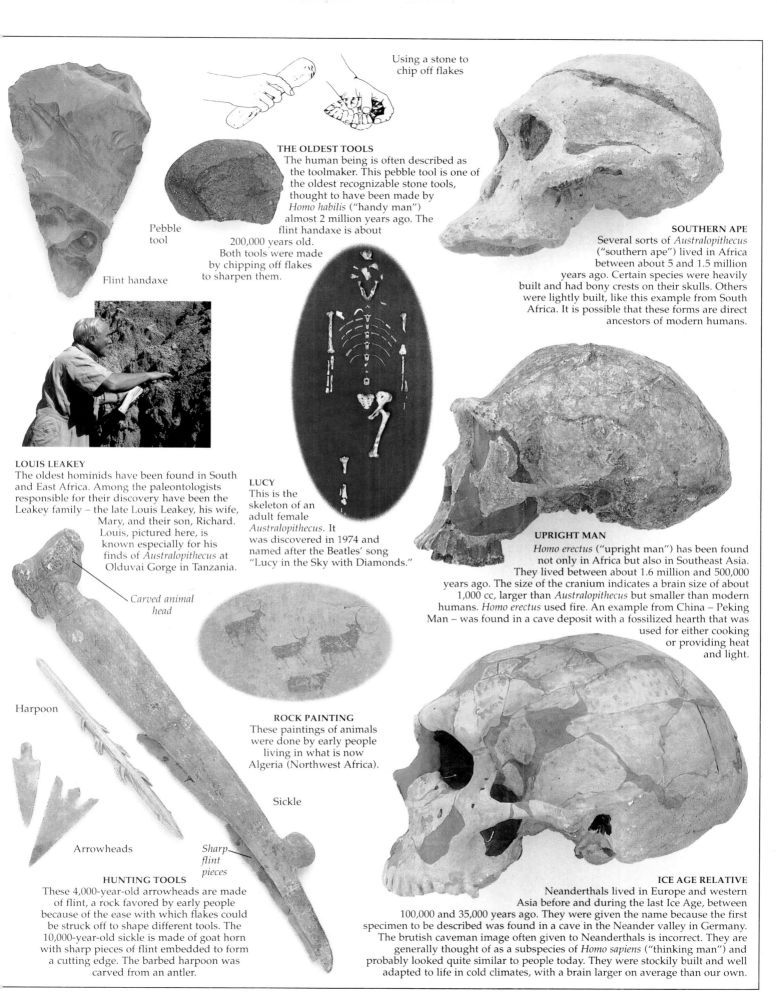

Living fossils

FOSSILS SHOW US that animals and plants have changed enormously since life on Earth began. Some have changed so much that modern species are very different from their fossil ancestors. At the other extreme, there are animals and plants living today that are almost identical to fossils millions of years old. The most striking examples of these "living fossils" are those animals and plants which are rare nowadays, such as the coelacanth and slit shells, which were known as fossils before they were discovered to be still living. Among plant species which have survived up to the present day are the horsetail (pp. 36–37) from the Devonian, the monkey-puzzle tree (pp. 36–37) and the ginkgo from the Triassic, and the magnolia, one of the earliest true flowering plants, from the Cretaceous.

LAST SURVIVOR
The tuatara is the only living survivor of a group of reptiles that were abundant during Triassic times. It looks like a lizard but its skull has a different bone structure. The tuatara lives only on a few islands off New Zealand.

Fossil horseshoe crab

FALSE CRABS
The modern horseshoe crab *Limulus* is not a true crab but is related to the spider and the scorpion. It lives close to the shoreline in the Far East and in the Atlantic Ocean off North America. It is very similar to the fossil *Mesolimulus,* an animal that lived in the sea about 150 million years ago. Other fossil horseshoe crabs include species that lived in freshwater swamps 300 million years ago.

Modern horseshoe crab

ANCIENT INSECT
Still common today, cockroaches, together with dragonflies, are among the oldest of all insects and range back to the Carboniferous. Some fossil cockroaches closely resemble modern species.

Modern cockroaches

Fossil cockroach

Ginkgo *leaf*

Fan-shaped leaves

Fossil *Ginkgo*

LONE RANGER
Ginkgos first appeared in the Triassic and were much more widespread in the past than they are today. Only a single species, *Ginkgo biloba*, lives today. Ginkgos are hardy trees that grow naturally in the forests of western China but can also be seen in many cities around the world because they are not easily hurt by pollution. The characteristic fan-shaped leaves are easily recognizable when fossilized, as in this Jurassic example.

Modern *Ginkgo* branch

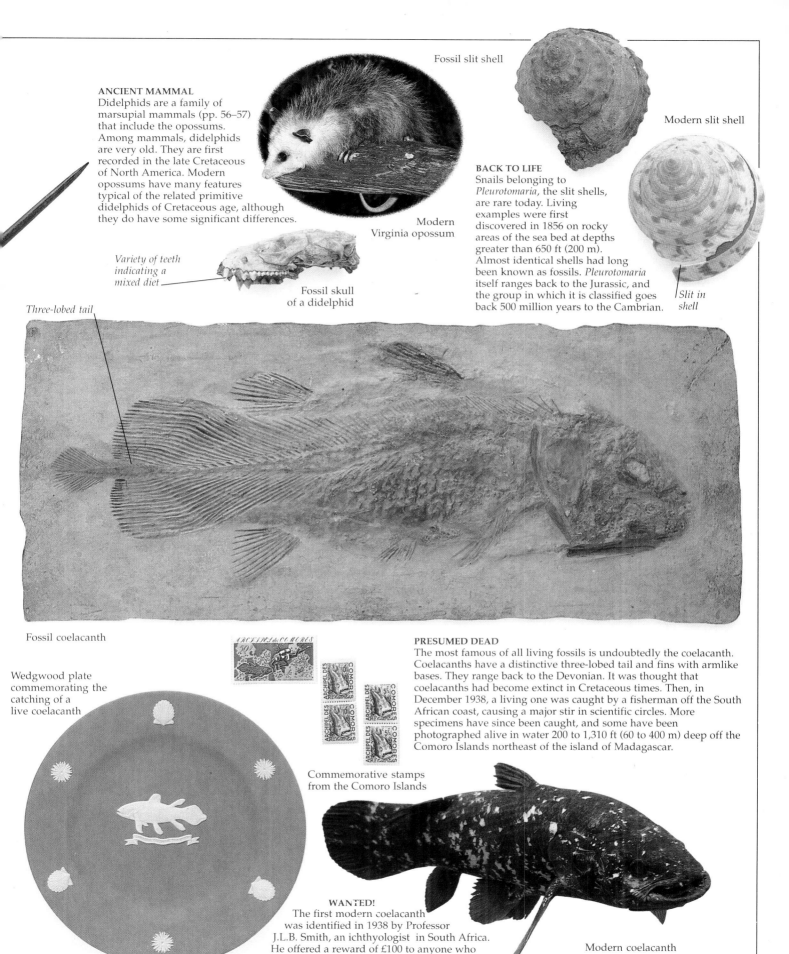

ANCIENT MAMMAL
Didelphids are a family of marsupial mammals (pp. 56–57) that include the opossums. Among mammals, didelphids are very old. They are first recorded in the late Cretaceous of North America. Modern opossums have many features typical of the related primitive didelphids of Cretaceous age, although they do have some significant differences.

Fossil slit shell

Modern slit shell

BACK TO LIFE
Snails belonging to *Pleurotomaria*, the slit shells, are rare today. Living examples were first discovered in 1856 on rocky areas of the sea bed at depths greater than 650 ft (200 m). Almost identical shells had long been known as fossils. *Pleurotomaria* itself ranges back to the Jurassic, and the group in which it is classified goes back 500 million years to the Cambrian.

Slit in shell

Modern Virginia opossum

Variety of teeth indicating a mixed diet

Fossil skull of a didelphid

Three-lobed tail

Fossil coelacanth

Wedgwood plate commemorating the catching of a live coelacanth

Commemorative stamps from the Comoro Islands

PRESUMED DEAD
The most famous of all living fossils is undoubtedly the coelacanth. Coelacanths have a distinctive three-lobed tail and fins with armlike bases. They range back to the Devonian. It was thought that coelacanths had become extinct in Cretaceous times. Then, in December 1938, a living one was caught by a fisherman off the South African coast, causing a major stir in scientific circles. More specimens have since been caught, and some have been photographed alive in water 200 to 1,310 ft (60 to 400 m) deep off the Comoro Islands northeast of the island of Madagascar.

WANTED!
The first modern coelacanth was identified in 1938 by Professor J.L.B. Smith, an ichthyologist in South Africa. He offered a reward of £100 to anyone who found a second one. He had to wait until 1952 before he had one in his possession.

Modern coelacanth

Fossil hunting

To find the fossil remains of a creature that lived millions of years ago is a thrilling experience. Fossil collecting is a hobby that can be enjoyed by anyone using the most basic tools. Sea cliffs, quarries, and other exposures of rock all over the world provide productive places for fossil collectors but safety must always be kept in mind. It may be necessary to get permission to collect from landowners, and attention must be paid to conservation - fossil localities can easily be ruined by over-collecting.

An historic find?

CHISELS
A hammer and chisel are valuable aids when removing fossils from their matrix (the piece of surrounding rock).

FIELD NOTEBOOK
The type of rock formation and locality of finds should be recorded in a field notebook.

HAMMERS
A geological hammer can be used to break up rocks.

Standard geological hammer

Hammer for use with a chisel

TROWELS
Fossils in soft sediment, especially sand, may be removed using a trowel.

GEOLOGICAL MAP
Geological maps are useful for locating promising places to collect fossils, as they help in identifying the age, location, and name of rock formations.

HAND LENS
A pocket hand lens with a magnification of 10 to 20 times is valuable for examining fossils in the field.

BRUSHES
Brushes can be used for brushing away sediment during excavation of fossils from soft rocks.

Safety helmet

Sieve for
separating
out small fossils

IN THE FIELD
This boy should be
wearing a helmet
and safety goggles.
Great care should be
taken when fossil
collecting. A helmet
is a must, especially
when working
beneath unstable
rock faces. Goggles
protect your eyes from
flying chips of stone.

Bivalve

Brachiopod

DRAWER OF SPECIMENS
After cleaning with water, fossils
should be stored carefully. Shallow
cardboard trays are convenient for
holding fossils and their labels. The
more care that is given to labelling a
collection, the more interesting
and worthwhile it will be.

Echinoid

Coral

Echinoid

Ammonite

Brushes and dental picks for
fossil preparation

MAGNIFYING GLASS
A large magnifying glass or a binocular
microscope is invaluable for close study.

BRACHIOPOD
Sphaeroidothyris
sphaeroidalis
Jurassic . Bajocian
Upper Inferior Oolite
East Cliff , Burton
Bradstock , Dorset ,
England

LABELS
It is important to label
specimens fully. Apart
from the names of the
fossils, details should be
given of rock formation
and the place where they
were found. Fossils can
also be numbered for future identification using gummed labels.

MICROSCOPE SLIDES
Small fossils can be kept in wooden or
cardboard slides, so they can be looked
at under a microscope. They should be
stuck down with a nontoxic,
watersoluble glue or secured beneath a
transparent glass cover.

Canvas bag for
larger fossils

ILLUSTRATED RECORD
It is rewarding to keep a
record of a collection
with drawings
and descriptions.
These beautiful
books record
details of fossils
collected over 100
years ago.

Plastic pots for
collecting small
fossils

Goggles

Index

Acknowledgments

Dorling Kindersley would like to thank:
Plymouth Marine Laboratory, National Museum of Wales, Kew Gardens for specimens for photography; Lester Cheeseman and Thomas Keenes for additional design assistance; Anna Kunst for editorial assistance; Meryl Silbert; Karl Shone for additional photography (pp. 18–19); Jane Parker for the index

The author would like to thank:
M.K. Howarth; C Patterson; R.A. Fortey; C.H.C. Brunton; A.W. Gentry; B.R. Rosen; J.B. Richardson; P.L. Forey; N.J. Morris; C.B. Stringer;

A.B. Smith; J.E.P. Whittaker; R. Croucher; S.F. Morris; C.R. Hill; A.C. Milner; R.L. Hodgkinson; C.A. Walker; R.J. Cleevely; C.H. Shute; V.T. Young; D.N. Lewis; A.E. Longbottom; M. Crawley; R. Kruszynski; .C. Bell; S.C. Naylor; A. Lum; R.W. Ingle; P.D. Jenkins; P.D. Hillyard; D.T. Moore; J.W. Schopf; C.M. Butler; P.W. Jackson

Picture Credits
t=top, b=bottom, m=middle, l=left, r=right

Aldus Archive: 53tm; 54bl
Alison Anholt-White: 28tl
Ardea: 9bl; 21m; 42m; 42bl; 43t; 61tm
Biofotos/Heather Angel: 26m; 31mr; 39br; 44–5bm, 60tr
Bridgeman Art Library: 14mr; /Musee Cluny/Lauros-Giraudon 17tl
Dept. of Earth Sciences, University of Cambridge: 39mr
Cleveland Museum of Natural History, Ohio: 59m
Bruce Coleman: 8br; 22m; /Jeff Foote 28tr, 39m, 40m, /Fritz Prenzel 57br; /Kim Campbell 59ml
Simon Conway Morris: 20m
Mary Evans Picture Library: 13ml; 14br; 15tl; 20m; 48t; 52tl; 54t; 54br; 55t; 55mr; 55b; 62m

Vivien Fifield: 50bl
Geological Society: 46t
Geoscience Features Picture Library: 9tr; 51tl; 51tm; 51tr
David George: 25m
Robert Harding Picture Library: 21br; 29m; 59b
Michael Holford: 12tl
Hutchison Library: 24tl; 57mr
Mansell Collection: 26t; 40b
Oxford Scientific Films: 44bl; 53bm
Planet Earth Pictures: 32ml; 41m; 43ml; 44mr; 63tl
Ann Ronan Picture Library: 15tm; 50br
Science Photo Library: 58r
Paul Taylor: 19b
ZEFA: 20–21bl

Illustrations by: John Woodcock, Eugene Fleury
Picture research by: Kathy Lockley